SECRET STREAM

COUNTRY LANES BOOK 1

SHIRLEY HEDRICK WILLIAMS

FIRE and GRACE
Publishing, LLC

FIRE & GRACE PUBLISHING, LLC

In memory of Mrs. Davis,
my Sixth Grade Teacher who inspired me to write.
I will always be grateful.

And for Tootsie, Mike, and beloved Roscoe.
I cherish the time I spent with you.

CONTENTS

CHAPTER 1

L ooking out the front window toward the road, Braedon Moore felt excitement and dread, expecting Charity to arrive at his house. Excitement because he hadn't seen his childhood friend since her mother's funeral where she had been surrounded by many relatives and friends who had come from various states to support her through grief. Dread, because he had realized as he hugged her that they were no longer kids. She was now a woman - a beautiful woman - and he, a man.

Both had lived lives away from their childhood homes, both had begun careers – she, employing her love for journalism in newspaper work and he, taking his passion for photography into the world of portraits. Neither appeared satisfied, even if a field was lucrative. Each married where their lives had led them though she had chosen to keep her maiden name for professional reasons, and each knew the joy of having a child. Strangely enough, each had suffered the painful loss of a spouse to death. They had always had much in common. Now was no different. Their mothers were gone, and both had come home to West Virginia to take care of properties. There was one exception to their commonality, though. Braedon had a sister he needed to guide until she graduated from college, and Charity was an only child... But no longer a child, he mused. What a poignant reunion they could experience!

Charity's dog, Punkin, rooted his nose up under Braedon's hand. He stooped down and stroked the white streak running down to the dog's black, moist nose. He scratched behind the German Shepherd-Collie's ears and ran his hand over the brown fur on his back before giving him a friendly pat. The dog sat down and raised a white paw for a shake from his second favorite human before standing back up to paw the man's blue jeans and nuzzle his plaid shirt. Head to head, they looked into each other's eyes. "You sense she's coming home, don't you, boy? I'll miss you. Oh, I'll see you from time to time, but I'll miss your companionship in my house." Ruffling the fur on the canine's white chest, he said, "Come on, let's go into the kitchen and get something special for you to eat." Punkin's white-tipped tail wagged, and his nails clicked on the bare wooden floorboards as he followed Braedon in expectation.

"Hello?" Charity Payne's voice called through the house.

Holding a dishcloth, Braedon came out of the kitchen to see her closing the front door.

"I'm sorry, Bray. I knocked, but no one answered."

Suddenly seeing Charity's strawberry blonde hair was like seeing the sun burst through the clouds. "That's fine, Charlie. Don't worry about it." He looked around her. "Did you see Punkin? I let him out the back door just a couple of minutes ago."

"No. I can't wait to see him!" Her face glowed with excitement.

"He probably headed for the woods in back. Let's go search him out."

The two walked through the kitchen and out the back door onto the deck Braedon had built for his mother. As Charity started down the steps, Punkin shot out of the woods. Both started running toward each other like they did when she was a teenager. As he jumped toward her, she grabbed him around the neck. Falling backward, she looked up at him standing over her in triumph, panting as though he were laughing. She, herself, was laughing up at him. "Okay, boy, you win!" He moved aside, thumping her with his tail as she stood up, brushing grass and bits of dirt off her black slacks and red blouse.

"Are you ready to go home, Punkin?" She rubbed the top of his brown head, examining the white streak down his nose, his white chest, and his white feet. "Wow, I've missed you so much, boy. That little stuffed dog could never take your place."

Nine-year-old Adrianna Douglas rounded the corner of the house. "They have a swing on their front porch, Mom."

"We have rocking chairs on our front porch, little girl!" Charity grinned as her daughter made a pretentiously pouty face.

At the sound of Adrianna's voice, eight-year-old Willow bounded out of the house. "Hey, I didn't know you were here, Anna! Everyone was so sad after your grandmother's funeral all we got to do was talk then. How long you gonna stay this time?"

Adrianna swished her cocoa brown ponytail. "Forever, if I have my way!"

"Yay!!" Willow swept her red hair up in glee, and it splayed in tendrils around her face when it fell to her shoulders.

"Whoa, Adrianna! I said we would probably be here for months, not years, and certainly not forever," Charity light-heartedly reprimanded.

"Say what you will, Mom. This is the place for you and me!"

"Can Adrianna come up to my room?" Willow's puppy-dog eyes pleaded with Charity.

"I suppose, but only for a little while. We have unpacking to do and then have to run to the grocery store before dinner," Charity said.

Adrianna's hazel eyes gleamed as she jumped up and down with pleasure.

As the girls ran through the back doorway and bounded up the stairs, Braedon grinned at Charity. "Come on in, and I'll make us some coffee. Do you still take yours with cream and no sugar?"

She grinned back. "Yes, and I bet you still take your coffee black. Right?"

"Guilty as charged," he said, waiting for her to enter the kitchen first.

She walked through the doorway with Punkin on her heels. Going around the kitchen table, she sat down, looking around at the blue walls and oak cabinets. "You painted."

"Yes, I had to make some changes so I could remain here without constant reminders. I was seeing Mom everywhere I looked. I missed her so much it hurt to stay here." Busy putting the coffee on, he stopped before placing the basket back into the pot. "I'm sorry, Charlie, that was thoughtless of me. I know your loss is fresh, and you must be hurting as much as I did."

"That's okay, Bray. I'm hurting, but seeing our old yellow frame house actually comforts me. I don't want to change anything yet."

"Given time, you will. You'll want to make it your own, with your own touches."

"Oh, I won't stay that long." She looked away with tears filling her blue eyes. She reached up a hand to wipe the tears before they could fall. "Then again, I don't know if I can part with the house. It holds so many memories of Mom and Dad for me. It will take time, that's for sure." She shook the subject closed. "I'll have a quick cup of coffee with you, and then, I've got to settle our things at the house and probably make a trip to the grocery store depending on what Mom still has left in the cabinets."

Braedon brought his fist down playfully on the counter and ran a hand through his dark hair. "I don't know what's happened to my manners today. You and Adrianna have supper with us. I promise it won't take long. I plan to grill chicken, and it's already thawed out. I can mash potatoes faster than anyone you've ever seen." When a negative expression crossed her face, he added, "You don't want to go to the grocery store hungry. You'll buy everything in sight. And I know you're hungry after driving all that way."

"Actually, Adrianna and I stopped at a rest stop and picked up a couple of snack crackers, candy bars, and orange juice from the vending machines." She observed the disappointment on his face. "But we both probably could and should eat some food. That's why I was going to the store. Mom left some items in her cabinets, though. If we eat here, I can wait until tomorrow to drive to the store."

"Terrific. I'll get busy with the grill."

"How 'bout I peel potatoes?" she offered.

"After driving all those miles from Ohio, I don't want you cooking or anything."

"I wouldn't be cooking. It might make me feel useful to do something. Better than just sitting here, letting you do all the work."

He didn't argue with her logic, but surrendered a smile. After setting two pans and a small bag of potatoes with a peeler in front of her, he grabbed the grilling tools off the hooks near the stove and went out back to prepare the grill. Later, with the green beans cooked and the potatoes mashed and fluffed up with milk and butter, he placed his homemade biscuits in the oven. "Won't take long now."

"That's what you said almost an hour ago," she laughed.

He rolled his dark eyes. "Well, these things take time!" They both began laughing so loudly that it drew the girls' attention.

"What's going on in here?" Adrianna demanded to know.

Charity took on a mysterious persona. "The enigma of time, my dear."

"Uh?" Willow looked confused.

"Never mind. Let's just sit down and eat," Braedon instructed.

With everyone seated, Braedon bowed his head to say grace over the food, thanking God for Charity and Adrianna's safe trip and company. When Willow said a big *AMEN* to the last sentence, everyone smiled and repeated, "Amen."

"Hey, Bray, where is your sister, Olivia?" Charity inquired.

"She's in Huntington. She has her own tiny one-room apartment with a kitchenette near the campus instead of a dorm room, but she's a sophomore at Marshall there."

"Oh? Not West Virginia State University? I thought WVSU was a family tradition around here."

"She attended there for a while, but wanted to join her friends going to Marshall." He passed the biscuits around for the second time. "I'm picking her up tomorrow morning to spend her break here at home. So you'll see and probably catch up with her a little more."

Charity smiled, "I'd like the opportunity. It's been so long since I've seen her."

When they had finished their meal, Charity announced she would wash the dishes since Braedon had cooked. "You will do no such thing,

Charity Payne! The dishwasher is quite capable of doing that job, and drying the dishes, too."

"Oh, you have a dishwasher now, huh?"

"Yeah, and you do too. Alice bought one about six months ago." He grinned and nodded his head. "You washed dishes by hand the last time you were home, didn't you?"

"Come to think of it, I did! Guess I was in a daze. Well, in that case, I will help load the machine."

"Nope, you won't do that either. The girls will gladly load the dishwasher so we can take our evening coffee out on the porch and relax a little. Isn't that right, girls?"

Adrianna hesitated to answer since she had planned to join the adults in their conversation, but Willow spoke up, clearly indicating with her eyes that they should leave the couple alone. "Yes, Daddy, it'll be fun talking to Adrianna while we load the dishwasher."

Once out on the porch swing, Braedon and Charity viewed the sunset together.

He tried to initiate conversation. "Well, hon, we've had a few rough years, you and I. It's downright strange how our lives paralleled at a distance."

"Yes, very rough for us both." Charity grew silent as if in deep thought.

They sat gently gliding back and forth in the swing, sipping their coffee for a while, comfortable in one another's company.

"What happened, Bray? I mean, what exactly happened to your mom? I couldn't get away from work, and we didn't have a chance to talk with all the people in and out of the house after the funeral. Mom said Vera had an accident, and you found her."

He really didn't want to go to that dark place in his mind. Not with Charity on her first evening home. But he couldn't ignore the question coming from his long-time friend and former confidante. How could he tell her everything without bringing more sadness into her life? How could he tell her that depleted by circumstances and drained emotionally, he and his daughter, Willow, had left Virginia and temporarily moved back home with his nature-loving mother? His mother inspired and encouraged him with photography from the time he had held his first camera as a boy. He guessed he had hoped for fresh inspiration. Then that night, when he came into the cottage on the hill in Country Lanes after shopping in Charleston with Willow, the house was inexplicably quiet - too quiet. He noticed a light-strip shining in the little building where his mother kept her large potted plants through the winter. Assuming she was still working in there, he put his daughter to bed and went into his room, closing the door behind him. When his mom wasn't in the kitchen, putting on coffee and making her usual breakfast of bacon and eggs the next morning, Braedon looked for her on the porch, finally walking out to the little glass-enclosed building in the back. On opening the door, he saw her right away. She lay sprawled on the floor, dried blood on her forehead.

"Oh, no, Mom..." he had whispered as he bent over and shook her gently. Even at a glance, he knew she was gone. At first, he felt guilty for not having checked on her that night. He kept thinking, *Maybe I could have saved her.* Old Dr. Kernshaw, however, informed him later that she had died instantly when she hit her head on a large stone pot setting on the floor next to a table.

I don't know the number of times I warned her about wearing those mule house slippers out of the house, he thought as he let his eyes wander off into a distant scene playing in his mind.

His vigorous mom didn't have insurance, and Braedon and his buddies dug a small grave themselves in an old family cemetery further back on the hill. She had often said she wanted to be cremated, and he allowed that, but placed the urn and other keepsakes into the space. His mother would have liked that, and he would have a place to come with flowers and perhaps plant a tree in her memory.

But all he said to Charity was, "Mom fell in the building out back where she kept her big potted plants and hit her head on one of the stone pots."

"I'm so sorry, Bray." She squeezed his hand. "So much has happened in our lives. We have a lot of catching up to do."

Both sat in silence again for a few minutes, but he felt comfortable with her by his side.

"How did your wife, Maggie, die?" Her direct question startled him.

He reminded himself Charity is a journalist at heart. "Aneurysm. It will be four years this April." Since she had dared ask him that unexpected question, he ventured, "How did your husband pass? I noticed you kept your maiden name."

"A heart attack two years ago. I kept my maiden name for professional reasons, which seems rather trivial in the face of it all. I lost both Mom and Adrian to heart failure. "

"I'm sorry, Charlie."

"I'm sorry you and Willow had so much grief. It doesn't seem fair."

"Life isn't fair. Life happens, the good and the bad." Braedon paused. Taking his eyes off the sunset, he turned his head toward her. "We live in a fallen and broken world, Charlie. It's only by God's grace and mercy we rise above the heartbreak."

Now they were both pondering thoughts of their own. The only sounds they heard were the squeaks of the swing and the soft flow of the creek as it ran by the front of the Moore land.

Charity spoke first. "It's good to hear a creek again."

"Yeah, it's peaceful tonight," he agreed.

"They buried our creek."

"By *they,* you mean the new business owners who covered it up with paved driveways and parking lots."

"Yes, and by *our,* I mean the creek near my family's property where our friend Cassie and we used to play. It's so sad to look over there and not see that familiar creek running its course through what used to be a meadow." Turning to him and changing the subject, she asked, "Have you been able to move on?"

"Move on?" He made an effort to consider this figure of speech. "Not yet, but I think I'm almost ready to build a new life now." Looking away as the blue twilight spread over the sunset's rosy glow, he asked, "And you?"

"I don't know yet."

"Maybe this round, I should grab you for myself while I can." He dared not take his eyes off the blue and gray wisps of clouds floating over the darkening hills.

Surprised, she shook her head. "No. We don't need to spoil our perfectly good friendship. Not after all these years, Bray." She, too, watched the wisps of clouds instead of looking at him. "Besides, we settled this years ago in our early teens when we realized we were too much like brother and sister to become sweethearts. Remember?"

"We were kids then, Charlie." He turned then and stared at her with penetrating eyes. "We're not kids anymore."

Charity suddenly stood up. "It's really time Adrianna and I head home. We have lots of unpacking to do and the house to check before bedtime." She paused in her steps to the screen door. Without turning around, she added as if it were merely an afterthought, "Thank you for a delicious meal, Bray. Guess we'll see you sometime this week."

Braedon felt disgusted with himself. *Now I've done it! I moved too soon. How stupid! I couldn't wait until she had even unpacked her suitcases! She needed time to heal and time to grieve. I couldn't give her that. She hasn't shared but this one meal with me in years, and I nearly spoil her first evening home by practically proposing to her.* He groaned.

She called up the stairs for Adrianna, and the girls came hurrying down into the living room.

"May Adrianna stay the night, Charity?" Willow asked.

"Not tonight, Sweetie. It's our first night back, and we need to unpack. But I tell you what, after we get settled reasonably well, you could come over and spend the night with her. How about it?" Both girls brightened at Charity's suggestion. "Come on, Punkin. Let's go home, boy!"

Soon, Braedon and Willow stood on the porch, watching the tail lights on Charity's white mini-van disappear into the deepening darkness. He leaned against the banister, one hand on a post, and lowered his head in disbelief at his earlier audacity.

CHAPTER 2

Charity looked through the windshield at her family's two-story frame house, built before the turn of the 20th Century. No light in the windows welcomed her home, offering hospitality and warmth. Now she knew her mother was truly gone. Her thoughts were abruptly suspended as her attention was caught by the sight of a dark human form running from the left side of the house, across the open field and into the woods, and Punkin's low growl. Deliberately keeping her imagination in check, she spoke calmly to Adrianna. *After all*, she assured herself, *it's probably a teenage boy taking shortcuts home at this hour of the night.* "Let's get our bags out of the back and set them on the porch. I'll shine my pen-light on the keyhole to unlock the door once we have all of them up there."

Adrianna, tired by this hour, merely nodded but obeyed her mother.

Only the moonlight, swaying in and out of gray clouds, illuminated the yellow house. Charity recalled that her dad, who had succumbed to cancer six years ago, had named the house *Old Yeller,* and she let a smile escape her weary mind. Her mother's favorite color was yellow, and after she had painted the kitchen the same bright shade, her husband put his foot down, sparing the other rooms of her *yellow fever,* as he termed her preference. Charity now looked forward to that familiar bit of indoor sunshine.

The Gourami fish in the sunroom's 40-gallon aquarium greeted her immediately with their need to eat, even though they rarely feasted at night. She switched on both the room and tank lights. Finding their food stored in the cabinet below their glass container, she sprinkled a little over the water. "You'll have to wait until morning for more, fishies."

The glare of the living room's antique chandelier glanced off the mirror above the white mantle and walls, hurting her eyes before they could adjust. The floral pictures graced the room with their usual loveliness. *They don't know the heart of the house has stopped beating,* she told herself. How deathly quiet it was in this house without her mother or all the people who had offered condolences.

When Adrianna carried more suitcases inside, Charity noticed the girl's red eyes. Flipping the switches near the steps to light the stairwell and the upstairs hall, she spoke soothingly to her daughter. "Honey, take only the bag with your pajamas up to the back bedroom and go on to sleep. We'll unpack tomorrow."

Apparently, Punkin had run around outside taking care of his personal business. Having followed the young girl inside, he ran through the house, wagging his tail in anticipation. Prancing back into the living room, his brown eyes questioned Charity.

"Sorry, boy. She's gone, and she's not coming back to this house."

He seemed to understand her words or her expression of resignation. When she locked the front door, picked up a duffel bag and headed for the stairs, he followed slowly beside her, rubbing his head against her leg as she climbed the steps.

"Well, Mr. Moore, it's nice of you to finally pick your baby sister up from school, even if it is before daylight. She's already missed a whole day of her break before graduation," Braedon's sister teased him while he was driving them home from Huntington in his truck.

Braedon's mind was still preoccupied with thoughts of Charity's return to Country Lanes. "So when did you start referring to yourself in the third person, Miss Moore? That's a bit demeaning, don't you think?"

Olivia flipped her dark red bob with one hand and tilted her head. "Uhh...since my big brother forgot to pick me up?" She winked a dark eye.

"I'm really sorry, honey. Charity arrived to take Punkin home and stayed for supper with us. Besides, you told me over the phone the other night you wanted to spend your first day straightening up your tiny apartment and packing for your break. Remember?"

"Charity? She back? Oh, wow. I bet Luna's fit to be tied or just plain having fits."

"Why's that?"

"You know she has had the biggest crush on you in like forever. She probably wants to run Charity out of town or strangle her!"

"Nah, Livie, if she had a teenage crush on me, which I doubt she did, that was years ago. Cryin' out loud, she's your age. She's grown now and probably involved in a real adult relationship."

Olivia zipped her black hoodie up and pretended to pick lent off her jeans. She squared her shoulders to look out the windshield at rays of daylight filtering through the darkness. "If you say so, Bray. But Luna didn't get the nickname Looney for nothin'. Keep that in mind."

Braedon frowned at hearing his sister dis a former classmate, but kept his mouth in a tight, firm line and gripped the steering wheel harder. He thought she would have outgrown her immature judgments by now.

Shafts of light shot across the queen-size bed, waking Charity from her deep sleep. Clad in the clothes she had worn the previous day, she rose reluctantly to a morning bright with sunshine. She almost stepped on Punkin, who lay on the floor near the side of the bed where she had slept. Scratching her head through a mass of tangled hair, she made her way groggily down the stairs, through the living room and dining room, turning right into the kitchen. The yellow walls sang of summer to her as she poured water into the pot and put coffee in the filter. Just as she pushed the button to start the brewing process, she heard a noise outside the window. Looking out, she saw a man's head duck down. Raising the window, she asked as roughly as she could muster, "Do you always lurk around our windows?"

Carter Grant's head popped up. "Oh, Charity, you scared me, gal!" A wide grin stretched his bony features. "I didn't know you were home yet." He swallowed so hard that his Adam's apple bulged. "I told your mom in the Fall I would take care of the property, and I was checkin' the hose here to see if it has a leak." He held up the nozzle almost level with his head of thinning hair.

"Did you not see my van parked outside?"

"No, ma'am. I came through the woods to the side of the house. Had this here hose on my mind since I left it attached through the Spring cold spell we had a while back. I figured it might have cracked and would leak."

"I'm sorry, Carter. I haven't had my coffee this morning. Would you like a cup?"

"Hmm...really?" His faded light eyes seemed fixed on his own thoughts instead of her question. "Don't mind if I do. Be right in."

"Don't bother. I was bringing my cup out to the front porch, anyway. I'll bring yours as well."

"Oh ok...good...thank you."

"Don't mention it. Would you like toast, too? I found some good bread left over from the gathering."

"No, that's not necessary. I already ate oats."

As she carried the tray of coffee and toast out to the porch, she decided to let her daughter sleep. Setting the food on a table between the rockers, she sat down, ready to enjoy the first taste of coffee. When Carter stepped up on the porch, she motioned to the tray with her mug. Just as he picked up the other cup, a black truck rolled into the drive, and Braedon hopped out. Hoisting a large bag over his shoulder, he ambled toward the front steps.

Shifting the bag's weight off his shoulder and down with a thud just inside the porch, he announced, "Dog food." Punkin greeted him with a wag of his tail, but turned and lay in a corner. "Afraid I'll take you home with me, are you, Boy?" The dog gave an apologetic thump on the floorboards with his tail before resting his head on his paws.

Charity's eyes widened. "Oh, I assumed Mother had dog food here for Punkin."

"No, I took what was left in a bag to my house. This is a new bag."

"I can see that. What do I owe you?"

"Not a thing."

"Punkin is my dog, and I intend to pay for his expenses."

He sighed loudly. "Do you have to be so doggone obstinate?"

She raised an eyebrow. "Doggone, eh?" Her lips twitched with amusement. "I'm not obstinate, Bray. Just want to pay my own way."

"Well, neighbors help neighbors, and friends help friends." He glanced at Carter for affirmation. "Isn't that right, Grant?"

"Hey, don't drag me into this, Braedon! I'm just an innocent by-stander, mindin' my own business. I suggest you do the same," Carter replied.

"Well, this is a fine howdy-do!" Braedon acted miffed. "I come all the way over here to do a favor for a friend and get treated like an old shoe."

"Well, Old Shoe, would you like a cup of coffee?" Charity laughed softly.

"No need to get all nice to me now. You've already hurt my feel-ings."

Charity chuckled. "Some coffee might improve your disposition."

"You sure? It hasn't done much for yours this morning."

She gave him a wry smile. "Come on in and get yourself a cup."

"I bet Carter didn't have to get his own cup."

"Oh, all right! I'll pamper you this one time, Braedon Moore. But if you want a second cup, you'll have to fetch it yourself!" It felt good to laugh out loud.

"Fair enough." He pretended she had finally appeased him.

Holding the screen door open for him to haul the dog food into the house, she recalled his plans for the morning. "Thought you were supposed to drive to Huntington this morning to pick up your sister."

"I did that already. Before daylight."

"Bet she loved your timing."

"She's snoozing on the couch as we speak." He grinned mischievously, bringing a twitch to her own lips again as she shook her head.

Seeing Willow still sitting in the truck, Charity called, "Hey girl, how about some orange juice?"

The girl smiled ear to ear as she moved up the walk in long white shorts and a t-shirt and sat down on one of the steps.

A while later, after the two men and Willow had left, Charity took a long, hot shower and slipped on a fresh pair of gray slacks and a long matching t-shirt. Standing in Adrianna's bedroom doorway, she raised her voice in lilting tones, "Rise and shine, Adrianna! We have just enough time for you to shower and eat a little toast before we drive to the store."

Adrianna threw her comforter back, pushed herself up, and swung her legs over the edge of the bed. "What are we having for lunch?"

"Whatever looks good at the store. But you still have to eat at least a breakfast toast," Charity insisted. "I'm laying a pink capri set out for you. Make it as quick as you can, okay?"

"Okay, Mom."

As Charity started for the stairs, she stopped at her mother's bedroom. Putting her hand on the doorknob, she pushed the door open and looked around the quiet room. The king-sized mahogany bed her dad had selected dominated the room and still looked freshly made with its white coverlet and the quilt folded at the foot. The large dresser was too neat to suit her. She thought there was no sign of familiar life in this room until her vision took in her mother's desk at the end of the room in front of a window. Papers littered it and stuck out of the top and middle drawers, open at different lengths. The bottom drawers were pulled completely out. *Did I leave the desk in this kind of a mess when I searched for Mom's documents?* She wondered and tried to recall the day she was forced to swallow her emotions at the loss of her mother and find the papers. She did suppose it was possible since her heart had been broken and her mind was trying to focus on the dreadful business at hand. Quickly taking charge of her mental meanderings, she strode across the room to straighten the desk. But she noticed two big muddy boot prints ground into the floor in front of the desk. She reasoned that there were people all through the house the afternoon of the funeral, but still... A *muddy boot print*? When her mind kept straying back to her mother's room and desk while she let Punkin out and in one more time, she decided to call Officer Bertrand, one of her mother's friends in the police department.

Adrianna stood open-mouthed and big-eyed as the officer looked at the boot prints and desk.

Charity felt she owed the officer an explanation concerning the desk. "I cleared everything off the top of the desk and straightened the drawers as much as I could. Remembering all the people that were in and out of the house, using the toilets and sinks, and my state of mind in looking for documents, I dismissed the mess and the prints. But then, I remembered everyone was dressed for the funeral service. I'm pretty sure no one was wearing muddy boots." A headache started nagging her as she continued her rambling explanation. "Besides, it's unlikely I would leave a mess like that in my mother's room since I would consider it disrespectful after she had just passed."

Officer Kerry "Bert" Bertrand's true blue eyes met her's as sincerity deepened his voice. "I'm really sorry about your mother's passing, Charity. As you may remember, I was here the day of her funeral, and there were a lot of people in the house and on the grounds. Most wore dress clothes, but some wore what you call casual. There were probably a few who wore some type of boots –ankle, mid-calf, and such. Why they would be muddy, however, beats me."

"Thank you, Bert – uh...Officer Bertrand. It was a confusing time for me."

"I have to commend you, though, Charity. You stayed composed if somewhat dazed." His eyes scanned the desk and room again. "Are you missing anything?"

"Not that I know of. I feel awful taking you away from your duties for something I'm not sure is actually a break-in."

"That's okay. You can't be too careful these days. If anything else occurs, call us...or, if you need anything, be sure to call me."

"Will do. Thank you, again."

He tipped his hat and quickly left, passing a still stupefied nine-year-old girl.

As they descended the stairs, Adrianna found her voice and squealed at her mother. "Why didn't you tell me you called the police, Mom?! I felt like an idiot trying to make sense of what the two of you were talking about and what was wrong!"

"Sorry, Honey. I should have shown you the mess on the desk and the boot print. I just didn't want to scare you."

"Well, waiting for me to find out the policeman is here 'cause there's a problem scares me more."

"Sorry. Guess I wasn't considering how you would feel when I decided to call him. I think I just wanted some reassurance that there was nothing to worry about."

"Well, I didn't see the mess around the desk. But I didn't see anyone here with muddy boots either." Her daughter eyed Charity's thoughtful expression.

CHAPTER 3

D riving past the car dealership which had buried the creek under their paved drive, Charity discovered the parking lot to the new grocery store, on the main strip of road leading to the town of Country Lanes, was almost filled to capacity with vehicles. She parked at the very end, and she and Adrianna enjoyed the soft breeze on their walk across the lot to the store. Having finally obtained a buggy, they made their way around shoppers and through the store to the meat aisle.

"Charity?" The voice behind her sounded incredulous.

"Yes?"

"Hey, girl, it hasn't been *that* long since we've seen each other!"

"Cassie Collins! Sorry, I've just had so much on my mind lately."

Cassie, tanned, with streaks of blonde in her light brown hair from a visit to a beach, smiled broadly. "I understand, my friend. But now you'll have to take one day at a time like I always do. This attitude of mine or philosophy or whatever you call it sees me through the days, weeks, and months." Her hazel eyes sparkled green and gold as she winked.

"*You,* Cassie?! We have a lot of catching up to do."

Cassie nodded and looked at Charity meaningfully. "We sure do! Call me soon."

"I'll do that!" They hugged before separating, each going their own way.

"Well, look who's back." A deep, male voice announced. "I thought we'd seen the last of you."

This time, she braced herself and turned expectantly. It was Roy Galligher, who maintained the façade of being easy-going and friendly, but in recent years, possessed neither of those affable traits. She remembered he had worried her mother over property rights, claiming that an old paper he had found states the boundary line includes some of her Dad's acreage inherited throughout the family's generations.

"Hello, Roy. How are you doing?"

He took off the black-rimmed glasses and swiped a hand over dark blue eyes and sun-spotted forehead below his receding graying hairline in consternation. Though a little stouter, he looked as neat as ever in the navy blue work clothes he preferred – she'd never seen him dressed any other way, no matter what kind of work he did. He answered her with a sigh. "Oh, all right, I guess. Just tryin' to figure out a way to settle this property thing since your mother died."

"I'm sure those property lines were settled by our ancestors years ago, Roy."

"I'm not so sure, but I'm lookin' into it for my poor ol' dad's and sister's sake."

"Well, do what you have to do. I really must get on with my shopping, and go home in time to fix lunch for Adrianna. Nice seeing you, Roy."

"Yeah, you go ahead with your shopping, Charity. We'll talk later."

She turned her buggy away, gritting her teeth. *Not if I can help it,* she thought. *The sad part of this whole business is that we were all friends before you found that silly paper.* There had been many winter evenings when he would drop by their house and spend a couple of hours visiting in the warmth of the living room, snacking on the cookies or pieces of cake her mother had baked and drinking cups of coffee with her parents. They had always looked forward to his visits and enjoyed his company. Then, after her dad died, Roy changed almost overnight after finding the paper. At first, he introduced his discovery to her mother and her one afternoon casually when she was home from Ohio for a weekend visit. After that, he kept pressing her mother to agree to help him legally change the boundary lines and fencing without argument or hassle. Yes, it was good to see him again, considering the years he had been her parents' friend and neighbor, and yet sad that she would now want to dodge him whenever she knew he was around.

She and Adrianna hurried home with the groceries. They prepared a lunch of cheese sandwiches piled with lettuce, tomatoes, and mayonnaise with macaroni salad as a side dish before unpacking clothes to hang in the closets and fold into drawers. The two spent the rest of the afternoon dusting, running the vacuum, and mopping the floors while listening to their music through their earbuds. When they placed a roast with quartered potatoes, onions, and carrots into the oven, Adrianna begged her to call and invite Willow and her dad over for supper. Thinking it might be good for her daughter to have company on the first day in her grandmother's house, Charity agreed.

When the doorbell rang, Adrianna flew down the two carpeted landings on the stairs, through the living room, and into the sunroom before Charity could walk from the kitchen, through the house to the door. "Welcome! Come in, come in!" The girl greeted them with wreaths of smiles.

Charity, laughing, invited her expected guests inside the house. "Yes, *do* come in!"

Braedon pretended he was amazed at this enthusiastic greeting. "Well, I don't think I have *ever* been welcomed as warmly as I am tonight!"

Willow walked into the room with a royal posture. "Don't flatter yourself, Dad. That greeting is definitely meant for me!"

"Oh... I guess I did jump ahead too fast," he conceded.

"I guess you did," Willow said sarcastically, grinning up at him. The father smiled affectionately down at his daughter, placing a hand tenderly on her head. The two girls giggled and took off for Adrianna's room.

"I guess I was put in my place," he joked to Charity.

"Don't feel too bad. *I'm* kinda glad to see you," she assured him.

"*Really?*" He raised his dark eyebrows.

"I said *kinda*."

Punkin scratched at the door and gave a short bark. When Braedon opened the door, the dog jumped up on him and licked his hand.

"Well, I guess I'll take what greeting I can get."

Chuckling softly, Charity motioned toward the kitchen. "Come on in the kitchen and help me with dinner."

"Sure. But are you asking a guest to help you cook supper?"

"No, of course not. I wouldn't think of asking you to help." She started walking through the living room. "I'm *telling* you." She looked back at him and made a face.

When they reached the kitchen, she pointed to a high stool. "Sit there and talk to me while I place the food on platters and set the dining room table."

"Oh, don't set the dining room table tonight, Charity. That's so formal. Let's eat in the breakfast nook. Okay?"

"Okay, if you think you guys will be more comfortable in there."

He nodded. "I do."

"Dad!" Willow suddenly appeared in front of him with Adrianna behind her. "You should see Anna's room upstairs. It's at the back of the house and, boy, is it *big*! Big and *long*!"

Busy with the platters, Charity remarked without looking in their direction. "That's because it's a built-in porch."

"That's why it has so many windows," Willow observed. "Dad, it has a full bed, love seat, coffee table, and a TV with a DVD."

"That sounds like an awesome bedroom," Braedon said.

Charity turned completely around to face them. "Yes, it is, and it was my room growing up. Since we live in a little apartment in Ohio now that I've sold our house, Adrianna sleeps on a single bed in a tiny room. So, she really appreciates more space."

Willow glanced at her dad's lowered eyelids and spoke up. "Well, I like my room and twin beds. And I can always watch TV in the living room." Her face lit up. "As a matter of fact, it feels good to have someone watching shows with you."

Adrianna nodded. "It sure does."

"Hey, girls, will you set the breakfast nook table so we can eat? Bray, could you bring the pitcher of iced tea to the table?" Understanding Charity's wave of the hand, Punkin, having taken care of business as quickly as possible outside in order to be near Braedon, now scooted under the table and lay down. The breakfast nook was, indeed, a comfortable room off the back of the kitchen. A convenient room, too, since the family room was just inside the white french doors to the right.

Soon, they were gathered around the table, holding hands as they said grace. The conversation turned to the changes in the area, the sights each wanted to see, and the things they wanted to do. "Tell you what," Charity continued with her wish list of activities. "I miss jogging along the roads here in Country Lanes. It's just not safe for me where I live now."

"The roads? They're busier now than in past years. It's safer to jog along the track at Shawnee Park," Braedon advised.

"Is that where you go?" Charity asked.

"At least once a week."

Willow piped up, "I like to swing on the playground while Daddy jogs!"

"Hey, why don't the four of us take a picnic lunch and go to Shawnee tomorrow? It's not too far," Braedon suggested.

Charity thought about it for a moment. "It would feel great to jog again. We'll all need to eat lunch afterward, and the exercise shouldn't take up the whole day anyway. I'm in!"

"Then it's settled?" he asked.

"Settled," she agreed.

While the girls were loading the dishwasher, Braedon and Charity took their coffee onto the back porch through the breakfast nook door. They sat contentedly in the redwood chairs, gazing out at the tall trees and the rock pond with its cascading waterfall. She spoke wistfully, "I'm always thankful for the peaceful sound of the waterfall and the ripples in the pond, but I sure do miss the creek."

He chuckled. "We did have some good times as kids, you, Cassie, and I around that creek. Didn't we?" he asked.

"Yes, we did. Do you remember when Cassie and I jumped in the deepest part near the old covered bridge in our shorts and t-shirts? And something kept sliding around, tickling our legs?" Charity asked, laughing out loud.

He began laughing, too. "Yeah, I'll never forget your faces when I yelled for you to get out of the water because y'all were playing with a water moccasin!"

By this time, they couldn't stop laughing together, and their daughters came to the door demanding to know what was so funny. When they recalled that time to their girls, they all laughed even harder.

"Oh my..." Charity said with eyes watering up and tears streaming down her cheeks. She could hardly talk without doubling up again. "I didn't think I would ever laugh again, and here I am about to split my sides!"

"Me, too!" he yelled involuntarily as the youngsters began laughing at the couple's behavior.

Winding down, Charity had an idea. "Say, why don't we ask Cassie to come jog with us tomorrow?"

"Yeah, if she's free, that could be fun...like old times." He grinned.

"Howdy, folks! What would be fun?" Roy Galligher spoke as he stepped up on the porch. His deep voice made the girls jump. When he saw their surprised faces, he offered an apology. "Sorry if I scared you. Rang the front doorbell. Guess you couldn't hear me for all the laughin' goin' on 'round here."

Suddenly Charity felt flustered, rose from her seat, and moved toward the door. "Won't you come in the house for a cup of coffee, Roy?"

"Thank you, Charity." Roy, pushing dark framed glasses further back on his nose, appeared pleased. "That's mannerly of you."

Settled with fresh cups of coffee in the armchairs, she and Braedon faced a seemingly relaxed man sitting on the sofa in the living room. "This has always been a cozy room," Roy began in a conversational tone. "All we need is the fireplace goin'."

His statement reminded her of the many evenings he sat here in this same room, discussing newspaper headlines and issues throughout the years. "It's really too warm for a fire this evening."

"So it is," he agreed. He removed his glasses long enough to wipe his eyes.

The room became noticeably quiet as they sipped coffee, each aware that the reason for his visit hung heavily in the air. Placing his cup and saucer carefully down on the coffee table, he took a deep breath. "Have you thought about my proposal to your mother, Charity? It benefits both of us. I'm actually offerin' you money for what really already belongs to me. Jus' wantin' to officially settle the dispute privately. You should want to rid yourself of those few acres. It would be less worry for your pretty little head."

At the last statement, Charity's posture straightened, and her body stiffened. "I don't mind worrying my *pretty little head*, as you put it, about my parents' property."

An audible sigh escaped him before he could control it or cover up the discouragement he felt. "So, are you saying *no* to my offer?"

They were staring at each other as if it were a stand-off. "Yes, I guess I am, sir."

"You'll regret this decision, Charity. I'll have to take it to court now."

"Do what you must, Roy. I'll do the same." Her voice held steady.

He jumped up, his temper getting the best of him. Pointing a finger at her, he shouted, "You're a foolish, silly little girl, Charity Payne!"

Punkin raised his head off the carpet beside Charity's chair and whimpered when he heard the angry tones from an old family friend.

Braedon remained silent through their show-down, but now set his cup and saucer firmly on a table and stood up. "I think you've overstayed your welcome, Mr. Galligher."

"Oh, I see!" The irate man declared. "*You* have a hand in her stupid decision! Well, I'm warnin' both of you right now! You'll both be sorry!"

"It's about time you leave, Galligher!" Braedon's eyes grew dark with intent. "Or do you need help making a quick exit?"

Spotting the girls peering anxiously around the doorframe, Charity's tone softened, "I'm sure that won't be necessary, Bray. Roy Galligher was brought up to be a gentleman and knows how to behave mannerly in someone else's home." Turning her head slightly toward the doorframe where the girls were waiting in suspense. "Don't you, Roy?"

Both men followed the direction of her attention. Braedon kept quiet as Roy stated. "Yes, I most certainly do." Deciding on a different tactic, he added. "I'm sorry I got carried away. Didn't mean to insult you, Charity. Just hate to see old friends have to go to court over such a frivolous thing. Know what I mean?"

"Yes, I understand perfectly. But it *has* been a long, busy day, and I think we should call it a night. Okay?" She suddenly felt completely exhausted, as though she had been running a race, carrying a heavy burden.

"Certainly," he agreed. Smiling as though it pained him, he said, "Guess I'll see you in court."

She only nodded and accompanied him through the sunroom and to the front door. He didn't look back as she said, "Bye."

Braedon came up behind her and placed a hand on her shoulder. "Well, we almost enjoyed a whole evening."

Turning around, she said, "I did enjoy the evening, Bray, and I'm sure Adrianna had a good time, too. For a while, we took a break from our loss and sorrow."

"I'm sorry it was ruined by Galligher's pressure tactics," he began apologizing.

"He didn't ruin the pleasant time we shared," she stated.

"He couldn't, could he?" Braedon whispered.

"Oh, he could have, but we have a choice, and we won't let him." She smiled.

He looked amazed. "You know, you're right. Thank the Lord."

"Yes, thank the Lord..." Looking deeply into his eyes, she knew there was a new understanding between them. "Umm... I wasn't going to spoil our evening together by bringing up a small worry, but I no longer believe it would mar our enjoyable time."

Braedon backed up. "And what worry is this?"

"Let me show you. Come upstairs."

Braedon looked at her through his eyelashes and raised his eyebrows.

Charity blushed. "*Really*, Bray?"

He straightened up. "Sorry. Definitely my bad, and I ask the Lord and you to forgive me."

She nodded and started up the steps. "It's in Mother's room."

When both stood outside the open door of the room, she told him about the mess on the desk, and all the drawers pulled out. Braedon listened intently and then asked, "You say you wouldn't have left the desk like that when you were looking for the documents?"

"Well...at first, I was shocked to discover such a mess around her desk. But then...I did tell myself I might have been in such a bereaved state and daze that the stress of searching for the papers overwhelmed me to such an extent I wasn't myself and..." She trailed off, reliving the day she had to cope with her emotions while gathering the necessary documents.

"So...why are you worried about it?" Bray questioned.

"Because I found these just moments after wondering if I had actually left such a horrible mess." She stepped into the room and pointed at the boot prints, outlined now in dried mud. "When I couldn't get these prints off my mind, I actually called the police. But I don't think

Bert...officer Bert... thought they were that important since we had so many people in the house after the funeral."

Braedon squatted, examining the prints. "Wow. They're too large for anyone living in the house. That's for sure. You didn't ask a repairman to check anything upstairs, did you?"

"No. No one. There's been no one here with this type of boots, large soles with grid, that is...well...not that I know of... This is what worries me."

Their eyes locked in great concern.

When Braedon and Willow left the house, Charity locked the door with the old key her family had used all her life. As they ascended the stairs, Adrianna squeezed her arm. "Thanks, Mom, for inviting them over. Willow and I had such a cool time."

"You're welcome, Honey. But Bray and I had a good time, too."

Adrianna gazed curiously as her mother's lips lifted faintly at the corners.

CHAPTER 4

S unshine poured into the bedroom the next morning as if its shafts of light carried the message *Good Morning* from Heaven's throne room. Charity opened her eyes and smiled, remembering they were supposed to go jogging at Shawnee Park. Expecting Punkin to be lying beside the bed, she watched where she stepped this time, but was surprised to see he wasn't there. She reached for her robe at the foot of the bed and walked down the hall toward her daughter's bedroom. There she saw Punkin, not lying beside Adrianna's bed, but in it! A gasp flew out of her before she could stop it, causing the girl to sit bolt upright.

"All right, you two. Rise and shine!! We go jogging today!"

Punkin' raised his head. Dog and girl looked at each other, mystified by the lady of the house laughing all the way down the stairs and into the kitchen. Charity hoped the Contemporary worship music wafted upstairs along with the scent of bacon and eggs. She wasn't disappointed when she heard both girl and dog bounding down to the breakfast nook. This morning its peach and cream-colored curtains lit by the sun cheerfully greeted them. It occurred to her that this room, too, had once been a porch, but now was transformed into a breakfast nook/laundry room, washer and dryer hidden by white folding doors.

"Cassie! Are you awake yet?" Charity held the cell up to her ear with one hand while the other busied itself with the metal spatula. "Oh, you sleepwalk and talk in your sleep?" She gave a soft chuckle. "Hey, throw your jogging duds on, and come grab breakfast over here. Bray and I want you to go to Shawnee with us. He says I'll like the track there, and the girls can play." She listened for a few minutes, and then interrupted her best friend. "No, don't worry about lunch. We're going to picnic there. Huh?" Listening again, she frowned. "You can't change the appointment? Well, I suppose I should be grateful you can eat breakfast and jog with me. Hurry up. The food is almost ready."

When she had taken food to the table for Adrianna, and dished out a little into Punkin's bowl, she ran upstairs to pull on her blue and white jogging clothes, socks, and white running shoes. She was ready by the time Cassie showed up in a mid-thigh white short set, and the two ate while Adrianna dressed. They were having coffee on the front porch when Braedon's truck drove into sight. He honked the horn even though it wasn't necessary.

"Ready to roll, gals?" Braedon yelled.

"All set," Cassie called back. "Where's Livie?"

"She still has unpacking to do and wants to lounge around the house. Think she's catchin' up on her sleep and leisure time."

"Well, tell her I hope to see her soon."

"Will do."

Punkin lay down on the porch and gave them a big brown-eyed apologetic look. Apparently, he wanted to stay home. Adrianna fetched a water bowl for him and promised they'd all be back soon.

Since Cassie had an appointment later, she took her little blue Beetle Bug, as she called her 2019 Volkswagen. Charity decided to let Braedon drive her van with her in the passenger seat and the girls sitting in the back. As soon as they turned into Shawnee Park, she felt enthused over the track, but fascinated by the mound there. Dressed in denim and t-shirts, both girls were ready to play and ran to the playground, but she wandered to the ancient burial mound and stood mesmerized by its shape.

"Hopewell!" Braedon shouted, striding across the expanse of green grass in his black running shorts and a muscle shirt.

"Beg your pardon?" Charity responded, unable to take her eyes off the site.

"It's a Hopewell, one of the ancient burial mounds named after a man on whose property in Ohio they were first recognized. It makes you wonder about the people who built it and what they really called themselves."

"Yes, it does," she whispered dreamily.

"Well, if you're interested, we could drive to South Charleston's Adena Mound sometime."

"I'd like that very much."

"The largest one is the Grave Creek Mound. We'd have to make a day of it, though, if we wanted to visit-" He stopped talking when her eyes widened, and she stared at the mound. "Uh oh, I can almost see wheels turning in your head, Charlie." He rolled a hand into a loose fist, bringing it to his mouth as he bent his head, cleared his throat, and peered up at her. "I've seen this expression on your face when we were kids."

"Yeah?"

"Yeah. You're working on an idea."

"Hey!" Cassie called. "Are we going to jog or what? Time is ticking!" They exchanged glances and sprinted toward her, and the three took off on the track, occasionally chatting as they jogged, happy they were together again.

When their childhood friend drove around the paved circle and out of the park, they began carrying the coolers with sandwich makings and drinks Braedon had brought in the van. The girls ran to the shelter as Charity spread the plastic, red-checkered tablecloth. Each picked out their favorite soda and fixed their own sandwiches. Ready to eat, they took turns thanking God for the day, the park, the friendship, and the food.

As the girls sat talking under a maple tree at a short distance and the couple started re-packing the food, Charity declared, "I feel so invigorated by the jog, I could climb a mountain! This is a perfect place to exercise, Bray!"

"I always think so, too." His dark eyes scanned the park as if he was envisioning another scene. "Every time I'm here, the name reminds me that a Shawnee Reservation once existed in this location."

Charity looked around, trying to imagine what it must have been like then. They both paused in contemplation. "So, these days, they call this area a Sports Complex."

"Yeah, that's what it is now."

Finally, she sat down at the end of the table, deciding to toss her idea to him. His back was to her as he leaned against a wooden post, still looking around. "Bray, I have an idea."

He turned with a lop-sided grin. "I *knew* it! I could see the machinery working in your brain. What is it, now? Surely it can't be anything that gets us into trouble again since we're grown up now."

"Guess I did get some really harebrained ideas when we were kids."

"Yeah, like the time you wanted to climb on top of cranky old Mr. Brown's barn roof and throw down green apples for us to catch."

"Yeah, I guess you would remember that incident. Everything would have been fine if it had worked out the way I planned. We could have gone down on the creek bank, rinsed them in the cool water, and enjoyed eating those delicious apples."

"Instead, Mr. Brown came after us, swinging a hoe. And he would have hit one of us too if you hadn't fallen off the opposite side of the barn right into a hog pen."

"Oooo... don't remind me. I was up to my chin in smelly mud. Those huge hogs would have gotten me if Cassie hadn't run around distracting them and yelling for me to get out! If I recall, you were busy dodging Mr. Brown's hoe at the time."

"Well, what's your idea? It can't turn out any worse than that."

"You think?" She laughed. "Okay, here goes. I'm playing with the idea of sending a query to an editor I met a couple of years ago to see if he would be interested in our doing a spread covering the mounds in our state for his new magazine."

"By *our*, I take it you mean the two of us. With both of us doing research, you writing, and I taking photographs."

"You got it."

"It's been done."

"Ah, but not by this particular magazine; and not with the slant we would put on it."

Braedon now considered the possibility. "Hmm... such an assignment could give us something to keep our skills sharpened while we stay in the area and take care of business. I suppose it could actually be a lot of fun."

"So, shall I offer our services to this mag?"

"What topics does this magazine cover?"

"Places of interest –historical sites and tales passed down through the ages."

"And this is a local publishing house?"

"In Charleston. It's so new the only reason I know about it is through this editor." She looked him in the eyes. "Well, do you want to try this project or not?"

"Yes, but we both need to agree on the proposal, including the money involved. After all, we both have little girls."

"I'll type the letter tonight, and e-mail it to you for your input before sending it to the editor. Okay?"

"Agreed. Hey, if we're serious about this proposal, let's drive over to South Charleston this coming week. I'll bring my Canon. We'll stop here for shots of the Hopewell, then drive on to the Adena. Perhaps the next day, we'll take a trip to Moundsville to view the Grave Creek Mound."

"Whoa... "Charity waved a hand then spread her fingers with the palms up. "You're moving awfully fast, Bray. First, we e-mail the query letter. If the response is affirmative and we agree on a contract, we research everything – and I mean *everything* – we can find on each one of the mounds. Only then are we ready to set out to photograph and write."

"Meantime, it wouldn't hurt to snap a few pictures." It was clear Braedon itched to get started on a project. "It's been a long time since I've shot landscapes, and I'll want to play around with the angles and the lens, you know, get the feel of the camera again...the one I left at Mom's."

"Didn't you have other cameras where you worked?"

"Yes, but they belong to the company. Besides, they are good for fashion or portraits. The camera and lens I kept at Mom's take great Landscape shots, but as I said, it's been a long time now since I've done anything like that."

"I can't imagine you've lost your touch, Bray. But, I believe once we do as much research as we can possibly find, you will have a different perspective about each of the mounds, and will take your pictures from various angles trying to capture the mounds as they appeared when they were first built."

"You may have something there, Charlie. Most of their tops were later leveled somewhat throughout the centuries. And one of the travesties is a whole line of mounds running throughout the area were leveled for residential homes and even a school. This could have been the second longest line of mounds in the United States and a tourist attraction."

"I remember Mom had a friend who attended that school, and he said boys were always digging and finding arrowheads," Charity informed him.

"I recall that, too. I'm not sure how we would treat this part of the article." He shook his head.

"I think we should interview Professor Joseph. He's retired now, but would enjoy sharing his knowledge with us," Charity offered.

"Yes, he would, Charlie. And we could visit the state archives and make some trips to the other museums, even those out of state. We would want photographs of artifacts found inside the mounds."

"I agree, but we'll have to be careful we don't run over our budget. We don't want this article to cost us more than we will earn," Charity warned.

"Or take us away too long from our properties." Braedon sat in thought for a few minutes.

She appeared to have made up her mind, but phrased her next thought as a suggestion. "Perhaps we should split up on some of our trips and interviews. This way, one of us could stay home with the girls and-"

"And go over the material when we're together," he interrupted. When she nodded, he added, "Excellent idea."

"Well, I have another idea."

"Eh?"

"We go home to Punkin and think about dinner. What do you say?"

Braedon grinned. "Do you mind if I play Frisbee with him like I did when he stayed with me? I kinda miss that, you know?"

"Sure. He'll love that, Bray."

When the four arrived at the house, Punkin's usual dance with a wagging tail didn't greet them as expected. He wasn't curled up asleep on either porch. Charity and Braedon called his name several times as they all began searching around the outside of the house and scanning the field out back. The girls took off through the wildflowers and tall grass toward the woods, but doubled back when a muffled barking sounded in the other distant direction.

"Mom!" Adrianna yelled, "Come into the field. We can hear a dog barking somewhere, but can't see him."

Charity and Braedon hurried to them, and they all stood still listening. Nothing. Then, Charity shouted out, "Punkin!"

A muffled bark answered.

Braedon picked up the shout. "Punkin Boy! Where are you?!"

The barking bordered on a howl this time, and they all followed the sound until they spied an old run-down, brush-shrouded shack Charity had forgotten even existed. Here, Punkin's recognizable bark intensified as he sniffed and snorted, frantically clawing at the pitted door. She ran to let him out, but a good-sized stick was wedged in the rusted latch.

Braedon worked it out of the old metal loop, and Punkin barreled out the door with barks and jumps for each one of them, anxious to tell them something if only he could. Braedon asked the question on the tip of his tongue anyway. "What in the world are you doing in here, boy?"

"What I want to know," Charity demanded, picking up a well-chewed ham bone, "*who* put you in here and *why*?" They each darted bewildered looks at one another.

As Braedon went to his truck to get the Frisbee, she started to unlock the front door and realized it wasn't locked. Swinging it open, she tried to remember if she had actually taken the time to lock it. Was this just a coincidence, or did someone close Punkin' in the shed and enter the home? "Hey, Bray, humor me, and walk through the house with me!"

He realized immediately that something wasn't right and that she didn't want to alarm the girls. "Sure, I've heard you writers are eccentric. I'll play along."

For the girls' eyes and ears, she smiled. "Thank you, Bray. That's big of you."

He whistled all the way through the house, only pausing when he would quickly pull a closet door open. He checked the back door to make certain it was locked. "All clear, m'lady."

"Thank you, Bray. And I mean it," she said. "I really couldn't remember if I locked the front door, and it wasn't locked when we came home. I wouldn't have thought anything about it if Punkin hadn't been trapped in the shed."

"I understand. Better safe than sorry, as they say."

They all enjoyed throwing the Frisbee across the side yard to Punkin, who ran and jumped up in obvious glee to catch it. Once he had brought it back to someone, he stood with his legs firmly set apart and his tail high and taut, ready to spring into action. Charity's heart melted affectionately at the familiar sight. *How I have missed him!* Her thoughts were distracted by the big, toothy smile on Braedon's face and the twinkle in his eyes when he waited to catch the dog off guard and threw the Frisbee in another direction. Punkin would somehow catch it in midair and prance eagerly back to the man. *I may have grown up with this smart fur-baby, but Bray spent almost as much time with him, plus they were inseparable just days ago. He is missing him now.*

Plopping down on the wooden porch steps, the two laughed and patted the dog, who was trying to push them over with his paws. "Okay, *okay*, Punkin, let me catch my breath!" She begged happily.

"Come on, Punkin; give us a break, boy!" Braedon began calming the excited canine down.

Having calmed down Punkin, Charity felt so good about having people around her the first few days at home that she suggested they invite Cassie over for a spaghetti dinner. "I wouldn't have thought it earlier, but I believe it's really doing me good to invite people around right now."

"That sounds great, Charlie! I'm actually thinking the same thing about myself. Go ahead and give her a call, and then we'll both start dinner." He handed her his cell.

When Cassie finally picked up, Charity invited her for dinner. "Well, I really like spaghetti, Charity, and I'd love to come, but Zak is home for a visit right now."

"Your brother, Zachary?" Charity asked.

"The one and the same," Cassie said.

"Oh, I haven't seen him for years!! Since we were teens! Where does he live now?"

"He has his own apartment in Charleston near the school where he teaches. But he often comes home on the weekends through the summer."

"Do you think both of you could join us for dinner?"

"Just a minute, and I'll check." When she came back on the phone, she said, "Yeah, we'll come, and I'll bring the garlic bread and brownies with me."

"That's great! I'll tell Bray and the girls to add two extra place settings. See you then!"

While Charity browned ground beef, Braedon chopped up onions and green peppers.

"Are you going to make your own sauce for this meal?" Braedon asked.

"Nope. I couldn't make it as good as this brand. It's delicious." She held up the jar as if she were in a commercial.

He sent her his lopsided grin. "I've never heard a woman admit something like that."

"Well, that's me, always full of confessions." She raised her voice an octave. "Hey girls, pretty soon, you'll have to put the game up and set the table. Cassie and Zak are coming over, and I want us to have plenty of room." Having heated the sauce on the stove cap, she took a clean cooking spoon off the rack above the stove and encouraged him to taste it.

"Well, it's my turn to confess," he teased as she arched an eyebrow. "This is extraordinary sauce, and I'll need to remember the brand."

She smiled and nodded knowingly.

When it was time to pour the spaghetti into the colander, she remarked. "Well, our company better get here soon, or the spaghetti will be too cold to eat without warming it up again."

"Well, I, for one, like cold spaghetti," he responded.

"Uh huh, that's one, Bray. The rest of us would like to eat a good hot meal. Is the cola cold, yet?"

"Thought you said you liked a hot meal," he teased.

With a smile, she countered, "Not the drinks." Whipping the dish-towel at him the way she had done when they were teens, she added, "Oh, you *know* what I mean!" Seeing her flustered made him laugh out loud.

Charity quickly mixed up a salad and set out several choices of dressing.

Cassie, still in her jogging clothes, and Zak in a WVSU t-shirt, sweat pants, and sports shoes, decided to walk from their mother's ranch-style home, down the road and across the field to Charity's house for exercise. As they approached the side of the house, they saw a man in a black hoodie straining to see through the dining-room window.

Zak bellowed, "Hey, man, get away from that window!"

Shocked by the sudden blast of a man's voice, the watcher took off for the woods.

Ringing the doorbell persistently, they couldn't wait to warn their friend about the man.

"You've got to be kidding!" Charity's expression held hope they would laugh and say that yes, they were joking with her. But that didn't happen. They both looked soberly at her and said they thought she could be in danger.

They watched as anger rose in red-faced Braedon like an offended wildcat, and he leaped toward the back door. Zak, unwilling to appear any less brave, followed him. Not seeing anyone around the house, the women observed them from the windows while they searched the perimeters of the wooded section, but found no one and returned to the house.

CHAPTER 5

While Charity warmed the buttered garlic bread in the toaster oven, the girls pleaded with her to allow them to eat in the breakfast nook so they could talk alone together. Considering the conversation the adults could have if the daughters ate elsewhere, she agreed. As she lit the candles, she felt Braedon's eyes on her, but soon became aware the other two were also observing her motions.

Joining hands, they bowed their heads as Braedon lifted them all in prayer and asked the Lord's blessing on the food. They each passed their plates around the table until everyone had a goodly portion of spaghetti and a salad in the bowls set on each placemat.

"What's wrong, Charlie? Did we forget something? The Parmesan cheese?" He questioned her perplexed expression.

"No, I just can't get that man off my mind. Who is it? And why does he want to peep in my windows?"

"He's a peeping Tom. That's what peeping Toms do." Braedon declared.

"They don't call them peeping Toms anymore, Bray," Cassie corrected him. "They call them stalkers or voyeurs."

"Ugh, I don't like the thought of them, whatever they're called!" Charity declared. "Just who around here would want the role of a peeping Tom-stalker?"

"Well, we could go through our lists of neighboring suspects," Zak grinned.

"No, thank you, Zak," she demurred. "I don't think I could look at them ever the same again if I started suspecting neighbors or friends."

Taking another slice of toast from the platter she offered him, he said. "Well, suit yourself, but *I* would want to know who was that interested in what goes on in my house." A lock of blond hair fell to his forehead as his blue-green eyes gave her an earnest look.

"Okay, guys, let's drop this subject, and allow me to tell you about the idea I've had for a project Bray and I can work on while we're here."

Zak set his fork down on his plate and put up both palms. "Oh no, not one of your ideas!" Turning to Braedon, he asked, "Bray Buddy, are you seriously letting Charlie drag you into one of her quote *"ideas"* again? Haven't you learned anything yet, bro? Guess you like walking blindfolded across a plank. Oh, that's right, that was *me*!" He shook his head while the others could hardly hold the laughter erupting in them. "Well, I learned my lesson when I broke my arm!"

"Zak, I was only ten years old then, and it was your idea to play pirates!"

"Yeah, but I didn't know *I* would have to walk the plank blindfold-ed!" With his vehement denial, all control was gone at this point, and laughter exploded around the table. Imagining them as kids again, and remembering their stunts in play, had even Zak joining in the hilarity.

Taking their after-dinner coffee and brownies out on the front porch, they sat in a semi-circle, hearing Charity's plans for the article on the mounds.

"Oh, this sounds like *fun*! Let us help, too, Charity! What do you say?" Cassie's high-pitched tone expressed her excitement. "I can help organize material and enter it into the computer for you," she offered.

"And I can assist Bray with photography," Zak said enthusiastically. "Look, we wouldn't be doing it for money, but for the fun of it. I don't go back to teaching until the last week of August."

"I don't either," Cassie said. "This project could occupy our time and give us information we can share with students." She and her brother nodded to each other.

Braedon and Charity exchanged glances before both exclaimed, "Great!"

Sunday rolled around, and Braedon, dressed in his charcoal-gray suit since he was to take his turn as an usher, drove to the small stone church a little earlier than usual with Willow, who was colorful in her yellow sundress and sparkling rainbow sandals. There the minister, Pastor Green, introduced him to a fresh-faced couple, Joey Jackson, with his dark curly hair and light eyes, and his wife Sara, a woman with long, silky honey-blonde hair almost the same color as her eyes. The pastor informed him that they were guests in charge of special music. He no sooner had shaken hands with the beaming tenor, looking robust in a silver gray suit and his petite wife wearing a pretty pink suit, when the first members of the congregation began arriving. He rather liked greeting each person, asking about family and current events such as birthdays, weddings, anniversaries, and children's events or how many fish someone caught during the summer. He spotted Charity and Adrianna before they made their way through the line to just inside the door, where he stood expectantly. He couldn't help but notice his friend's sky blue eyes reflected the light suit of the same shade. Adrianna's navy blazer and matching skirt gave her an older appearance.

"Welcome back, Charlie."

"You've already welcomed me home, Bray."

"I mean, welcome back to the church."

"You don't intend that greeting to have a double meaning, but it does."

He raised his eyebrows.

"In the city, we usually slept in on Sundays since the newspaper offices were always busy."

"You didn't go to church there?" He looked disbelieving at her. "What about Adrianna?"

"She visited friends' churches and attended their Vacation Bible School."

"Well, I'm glad you two are here today."

"Thank you, Bray. I'm glad to worship in my home church again and bring my daughter here, though it does feel odd without Mom."

He nodded in agreement.

When everyone was seated, he walked down the carpeted aisle and took his place beside the two girls and Charity. Though the youth usually went to Sunday school, today, everyone remained in the sanctuary for the special music. He could tell they were all mesmerized by Joey's voice and the words of faith in his songs. When it came time for the congregational singing, Sara stayed at the piano, and voices rose eagerly in worship.

At the end of the service, Braedon invited Charity and Adrianna to his home for a seafood dinner.

"Thank you, Bray, but I think we've already monopolized your time the last couple of days. Think we'll just lounge around the house and porch at home. Besides, I noticed Aunt Florie isn't here today, and I never knew her to miss church. I need to call, let her know I'm home, and check on her."

He grasped on to hope when she had slipped and said the word *home.*

Starting to turn away, she looked back. "This is our day of rest before the busy week ahead. We have a lot of research, interviews, and planning to do this week."

"No pictures yet?"

"I want you to know exactly what your pictures are representing, sir."

"I understand that," he said, and then paused. "But..."

"But you are anxious. Right?"

"Isn't that a good thing?"

"Not when you need to keep a cool head."

"Gotcha, girl."

"See you tomorrow morning when we plan our agenda."

"Looking forward to it."

The girls were disappointed, but would plan activities over the phone.

Once home, Charity and Adrianna decided their Sunday dinner would consist of a chicken salad. Tuning the radio to a contemporary Christian music station, they worked together preparing fried chicken to cut into pieces to put in the salad they would mix up with croutons. For the dressing, they chose sweet and sour sauce. While she stood in front of the gas stove frying chicken, she talked with Florie on her cell phone and learned that her aunt had just been so busy working in her yard she needed to rest. With assurances that her aunt was fine and would soon get together with her for lunch or supper sometime, Charity placed the chicken on a platter. When cool, she and Adrianna mixed the chicken bits into the salad and added the dressing. Ready to eat, they each poured their own iced tea. The enjoyment of just the two of them in the house and working together surprised both of them. Taking their food out on the front porch, where they had set up a small table and straight-back chairs, added to their simple pleasure. Bowing their heads in their own private prayers, they sat eating in comfortable silence, watching a soft breeze stir leaves on the trees bordering the property. Charity couldn't help remembering the sweet sound and sight of the creek flowing through the backdrop of the green hills. Her heart missed a beat as she allowed herself to reminisce. Later, Adrianna wandered out into the field with the dog, almost to where the bank once existed. Watching her skipping across the grounds with Punkin the way she, herself, once had done when he was a pup, a knot formed in Charity's throat but also made her smile.

Rising to go into the house for a cup of coffee, she heard music floating from the kitchen. She recognized the song when the voices began to sing the chorus as one of her favorites, describing the angels in heaven. It brought back memories of another time, another song. Returning to the porch with her coffee and her recollection, she sat in one of the rockers and looked up at the gradual spread of a rosy, golden sunset. She envisioned her mother busy in the kitchen that particular evening, listening to the song Beyond the Sunset on the same radio. Eleven-year-old Charity had stood in the dining room listening intently to the words. She now remembered walking through the living room and sitting on the arm of the loveseat in the sunroom, looking out the window at a lovely orange sunset.

When her mother passed her on the way to the porch, Charity had asked her what she thought heaven was like. Alice had paused, smiled, and said, "The Bible tells us it is a place of beauty where the throne of God exists and where angels sing praises to Him. Jesus said He was going to prepare a place for us that where He is we may be." She, too, had looked at the sunset.

"Do you really think the streets are paved with gold?" Charity had asked.

"The Word of God tells us that the streets in the Holy City are pure as gold, but, Honey, whatever heaven is like, it will probably be more beautiful than anything we can imagine with our finite minds. After all, we are talking about the place built by our Creator who created and designed the universe, the earth, and all forms of life." The wonder of Alice's words had filled her daughter's heart with longing to actually see Jesus and a desire for that spectacular place.

Now Charity rocked back and forth, her mind reliving that scene from the past when the thought occurred there was no one but her to recall the day and that conversation. Her own daughter's voice penetrated her musings, calling her back to the present.

"Mom, what are you thinking about so hard? Do you see the awesome sunset?"

A pleased expression crossed Charity's face. "Yes, I see that lovely sunset." Motioning to another rocker, she spoke softly. "Come sit down for a while, and let me tell you about a special song and a conversation I had with your grandmother when I was just a little older than you."

CHAPTER 6

The next morning, Charity was up early, showered, and dressed in blue jeans and a plaid blouse. While the coffee brewed, she sat on the kitchen stool at the counter, poured milk on her cereal, and began to eat when Braedon and Willow knocked at the front door. Holding her bowl and still taking sips from the spoon, she walked through the house. Opening the door, she said, "Good Morning! Would you two like some cereal?"

Braedon looked freshly groomed in his jeans and pale blue shirt. "No, thank you. We ate our cereal already before we dressed."

Beaming in a yellow short set, Willow asked, "Where's Adrianna?"

"Oh, she's on her way downstairs to eat breakfast. Let's go into the breakfast nook so we can sit down and talk." Charity answered. As they walked through the sunroom and living room, Adrianna bounded down the stairs in her flowered capris and pink hoodie.

While Adrianna ate in the breakfast nook, they all sipped orange juice.

"Well, are you ready to hear our plans?" Charity asked.

Braedon replied, "I thought you said that's what we would do today, make plans."

"I could hardly sleep last night thinking about our project, Bray. My mind started working on it earlier than I had anticipated, so I did too. I think we *should* drive to South Charleston and take a look at the mound there. What do you say?"

"Sure, I'll run home and get my Canon and equipment."

"No, it's not time for pictures yet, Bray."

Frustration in his voice, he exclaimed, "Charity, you can't expect me just to want to view the mound and not take photographs!"

When he raised his voice, the girls looked wide-eyed at each other, and Punkin moved restlessly under the table.

"Bray." Charity recognized her mother-tone of voice, the one she used when she calmed a child. "You are a professional photographer. The more information you have about the mounds and the better understanding you have of the artifacts found there, the deeper your imagination will delve into the past. I don't know a lot about photography techniques, but I am aware that you can present the mounds in such a way as to make them so intriguing a reader will want to read an article on them."

He visibly quieted himself as if he were mauling over her line of reasoning, and the room grew silent. After a few minutes, he nodded.

Leaving Punkin in the house this time and deliberately making sure the house was locked up, the four of them set out on the interstate for South Charleston in Charity's van. The girls in the backseat kept up a running conversation about new mystery books they had read while the adults were preoccupied with their own thoughts. Parking near a coffee shop Charity planned to visit later, Braedon emerged from the vehicle and opened the door for their daughters. Even before reaching the mound, they were all viewing it in wonder when they began to notice that people were busily walking past the site on their way to shop or enter restaurants, some milling around or sitting on benches talking to each other. They suddenly realized that these residents were accustomed to seeing this burial site, once held sacred to a culture long gone.

Walking around the mound, viewing it from different angles, they drew the attention of a passerby. The thought occurred to Charity that perhaps when the city inhabitants saw people gazing at the mound, they were reminded of its purpose and historical value. As the four examined the chart exhibited there, she told them that it was originally built by the Adena culture around 250 to 150 BC, thirty-three feet high, its top conical in shape but leveled in 1820 to erect a judge's stand during horse races.

"You've already started research, Charity?" Braedon's remark was both a question and a statement.

"I told you I could hardly sleep. So I pulled my laptop into bed with me and started browsing for information. Of course, I won't content myself with that. We will have to visit museums and interview people before I feel equipped enough to write a really informative article."

"Well, tell me what you do know now. We have to start somewhere, and I need to get a little closer to taking photographs. This is killing me."

"I know, Bray, and I'm sorry. But you will see what I mean and agree with me when we are ready for pictures. I promise you! For now, I know there were thirteen skeletons found in this mound, two at the top and eleven at the base. There was a very large skeleton in the center of the base, surrounded by ten others with their feet pointed toward him." Braedon and both girls listened in rapt attention, now looking at the base of the mound. "The skeletons were wrapped in elm bark and lay on white ash and bark. When it was excavated from 1883 to 1884, arrowheads, lance heads, shell and pottery fragments were also found."

"Mom, I have a question," Adrianna interrupted.

"Okay, shoot."

"Why would all those people die and be buried at the same time?"

"Well, at least for now, it's my guess that someone considered important by the native group died and, just as other cultures have been known to do, his servants were buried with him to accompany him into the spirit world."

The girls screwed up their faces, looked at each other, and squealed, "Ewee!"

Braedon grinned, and Charity cocked her head and grimaced when she nodded. "If this was the case and they were forcibly expected to do this, I would rather think they went willingly, out of loyalty and in peace, not in anguish. It's done, and we can't change the past, only learn from it."

With their minds now envisioning such a possibility, they all viewed the site with sober expressions until Charity shook her head. "There's a great deal we don't know about this culture, and I'm sure even the experts in the field of study ponder, so why don't we go over to the coffee shop for a break." She whirled around, pointing at the shop across the street and adjacent to the mound. "Hey, girls, remember the shop with the pictures of hot chocolate and various kinds of cookies in the windows beside the cups of coffee?"

The girls yelled, "Yay!"

"I could stand a coffee break," Braedon said.

"And I could enjoy a caramel latte!" Charity announced.

Charity, in old jeans and a long, white t-shirt, spent the next day going through her mother's belongings with Adrianna's help. It was a painful experience for her as the past rose up with each piece of clothing or item, making her smile in their clarity; and then shed tears when reality ripped through the fabric of memory. Taking only brief breaks to snack, it took the two of them most of the day to clean out closets, rummage through drawers, and box up everything. Once done, she looked around her mother's room at the bare dresser, chest of drawers, bedside tables, and all the boxes. Even the yellow and rose-flowered wallpaper couldn't lift the dark cloud of depression hovering around her mind.

"Come on, Adrianna. We'll finish this later," Charity said, throwing a dust cloth down in exasperation. "Let's go for a walk and visit Aunt Florie. I'm surprised she hasn't come by since we've been here!"

Adrianna, who had been curious enough about each object in the drawers to want to help her mother, was now weary of the task and ready for some fresh air. She swiped dust off her black capris and adjusted her flowered top. "Oh, I am *so ready!*"

With Punkin in tow, they set off slowly down the road, quickening their pace after a while to match the rhythm coursing through their bodies and playing in tune to the release of endorphins. Finally, they strolled along a winding path up to her aunt's house, which set on a knoll. As they neared the side deck jutting out over the above-ground cellar and started up the steps, they saw Charity's Aunt Florie sitting in one of the white lawn chairs. She wore a faded blue housecoat and slippers and was looking away from the visitors. When they stepped upon the deck, her big blue eyes grew even larger. "Charity Payne! Why didn't you call before coming up here so I could have baked something special for you?!"

"You know I've been home for a few days now, Aunt Florie. I'm surprised you haven't made your way down to see us. Surely you can see the van down there when we're home. I handed over mother's Geo Tracker to Cousin Kaye, but you should've been able to see the mini. Besides, Braedon and Cassie have parked their vehicles there from time to time, too." With a sweeping gesture, Charity looked down the hill toward the house.

Florie shook her head before pushing her sandy-colored bangs out of her face. "No, Honey, I've been in the house about a week now. This is the first day I've been able to step out here."

"Are you sick after all, Aunt Florie?"

"No. I pulled some vines away from the fence on the other side of the house. Well, it turned out to be poison ivy." She raised her right leg so Charity and Adrianna could see a blistering rash with salve coating an infected spot. "I didn't want to worry you, Honey."

"Oh my goodness, Aunt Florie! Have you seen a doctor? It looks like you may have come into contact with poison oak or sumac, too, maybe both!" Charity was appalled by an open, raw area.

"Only when it started spreading and the skin got infected." She heaved a loud sigh. "The doctor at Urgent Care gave me a shot and a prescription for antibiotics. I'm trying to remember to take them on time."

"Can I get you something? Do anything?" Charity asked.

"Yes. Yes, you may," she stated. "You could make us a pot of coffee and sit with me for a spell and tell me everything that's going on."

"I sure will. That's just what I need, too!" Charity pulled open the white storm door and started inside, but stopped to ask, "Oh, do you have anything Adrianna can drink?"

"There are cans of soda in the fridge. There are cookies in the jar on the counter too." Turning to Adrianna, Florie smiled and invited her to sit down beside her. Punkin plopped down at the girl's feet. "Oh, and Charity, get Punkin some water, too. He looks thirsty after his walk up here."

A sick feeling churned in her stomach as Charity made the coffee. It hurt her to see her aunt, usually active, in so much discomfort she didn't want to move around. Charity was only two years of age when her mother's younger sister, thirteen-year-old Florence, came to live with them. Her aunt went to Junior High and High school while she stayed with them before working in a supermarket, where she met and soon married Ben. Separation would have been difficult when Florie and her husband moved to Barboursville, Ohio if they all hadn't made trips back and forth about once a month. After some years, while Ben was on the job in a plant there, he suffered a stroke and never recovered, dying only weeks later. It was then that Florie moved back to West Virginia and bought a house near her sister with the insurance money. Charity grew up thinking of the woman as a sister as well as an aunt. She loved her almost as much as she had loved her mother.

Hiding her emotions, she handed Adrianna a can of soda, set a plastic bowl filled with water in front of Punkin, and then brought the mugs of coffee and a small container of cookies out to the deck. Sitting down on the other side of Florie, she looked up at an old one-story farmhouse on the hill above them. "Looks like Carter is taking better care of Mom's property than his own."

"Yes, he stopped painting or cleaning windows after his elderly mom died. It's like something died in him when old Mrs. Grant passed away."

"Wonder why he didn't tell you I was home? Or tell me about your leg?"

"Well, to be fair to him, I haven't seen Carter. If he did come over here, I was cooped up in the house and may have been taking a nap in the back bedroom. I really wasn't fit for company. Guess he had no idea my leg was this bad. After all, infection only set in recently, and I don't think I have seen him at all since my leg got so bad."

Charity nodded. Changing the subject, she asked, "Is there anything of Mom's you would like, Aunt Florie? I've been boxing things up."

"That must have been hard on you, Charity. I can just imagine. I could have helped."

"Not with your leg like this. Besides, it would have pained you even more than it did me since you grew up with her and then lived here with us while going to school. With all your talk of faith, I saw you stumble on the driveway." Florie's eyes rolled around to stare at her niece. "And when you entered the side door of Mom's house, you stopped and broke down in tears. I heard you moan, Aunt Florie."

"I really meant that about faith strengthening you in grief, Charity. The New Testament scriptures tell us that we, as Christians, don't need to mourn. And that is *true.* We have the promise of a greater reunion than ever recorded in earthly time to comfort us." Her gaze then shifted past her niece as she nodded her head in an admission of sadness. "But yes, I cried because our journey together here on earth had ended, and I knew I would miss her for the rest of my life." Tears filled Florie's eyes. "There *is* something I want."

"Name it."

"The broach. The gold letter A broach."

"It's yours, Aunt Florie." Charity leaned over and squeezed her aunt's arm.

"All right, enough of this." Florie swept away a tear with one hand. "Now tell me everything that's been going on with you and Adrianna besides cleaning out drawers. My friend Julia will come over for a visit in a few minutes."

"Your friend Julia?"

"Yeah. Julia Norton. She's a retired History professor. Down to earth and a big blessing to me."

Charity felt relieved hearing her aunt had someone around who cared about her. "Where did you and Julia meet, Aunt Florie?"

"Oh, she moved into that big old mansion Mrs. McGruegor used to own up on the hill next door to Carter."

"All alone in that big house with the round tower?"

"Yep. Well, actually, her brother, who is also retired, lives in the tower itself. You know it has its own kitchenette and bath. Julia says she loves the historical value and the architecture." Charity's aunt seemed to suddenly come alive with enthusiasm. " I took her a freshly baked apple pie one day to welcome her to the area, and we've been fast friends ever since. She fills me in on a lot of fascinating historical facts she says bores most people." Florie's eyes lit up. "But I find her information and stories totally exciting!"

They had a good visit the way they always had enjoyed through the years, and Charity felt at home finally. When it was time to go, she hesitated and bent down to give her aunt a hug and a kiss on the cheek. It was then she noticed the white starting to mix with the dark blond strands of hair at the temple. "I love you, Aunt Florie." She felt a deep need to tell her how much she meant to her since she wished she could have told her mother these words too.

Her aunt looked up at her with feeling pooling in her eyes. "I love you too, Charity."

Just as she and Adrianna stepped off the last step, a beautiful dark-skinned woman with lovely arched eyebrows and high cheekbones flashed a bright, toothy smile in her direction. "You must be Charity, the niece Florie is always talking about when I'm not forcing her to listen to my tales." The smile lit up her brown eyes, too.

"Yes, I am." Charity answered with a wide smile of her own. "And you're Julia, the blessing Aunt Florie declared. From what she told me, you don't have to do much forcing to get her to listen to your stories. She is as excited as a little girl on Christmas!"

The two women paused and shook hands, exchanging more pleasantries. "I ran into your friend, Cassie, in the grocery store, and she told me she is assisting you with an article on the mounds here in West Virginia."

"Oh, you know Cassie."

"Yes. I became acquainted with her when she would stop by to visit your aunt. Sweet girl. And quite intelligent." Julia's next statement sounded more like a question as she raised her eyebrows. "I told her to call me if you needed any help with it."

"You're a retired History professor, right?"

"Yes, and into archeology, too. My brother and I spent our summers on digs. But I won't bore you with details. You're probably anxious to go. Just want you to know I'm always available if you need any help with your project."

"There's no way you could bore me by relaying your experiences on digs or any information regarding History. They would actually delight me."

Julia's smile lit her face once again. "You don't realize how good that makes me feel. I'm looking forward to knowing you better, Charity Payne."

"And I, you, Julia Norton!" She hoped her own smile shone as brightly as this beautiful lady's.

On the way home, she and Adrianna slowly walked the trail, choosing not to hurry, but to bathe themselves in the glow of the golden sunset spreading across the sky. Suddenly, Punkin veered off the trail and took off into the woods. "Punkin!! Punkin!!" Charity yelled with

Adrianna's voice blending with her own. At first, they didn't know whether to keep moving toward their house or wait for him. After a few minutes, it became clear that he wasn't in sight.

"Well! I guess he can find his way home," Charity declared.

Adrianna frowned. "He *better!* Or I won't sleep tonight!"

CHAPTER 7

Braedon had worked hard, scrubbing the wooden floors, and still, he felt he wasn't as tired as he had hoped. He had lived alone, without his mother, for some time now since his sister left for college, and the house never seemed this quiet when Willow would stay up in her room reading her many books. He knew he had not felt truly alone for quite some time because Punkin had been with him. He had even talked to him, and the dog had wagged his tail as if he understood. Now, he missed his furry friend and the intelligent brown eyes. He missed sitting in the porch swing with the dog stretched out like a person, resting his head on Braedon's denim-clad lap. The evenings had been quiet and peaceful, and Punkin would make him smile with contentment.

Wringing the mop out in the galvanized bucket, he heard a heavy thud on the front porch. Puzzled, he went to the front door, opened it, and looked out. There sat Punkin with his mouth open and his tongue stuck out as if laughing, his eyes gleaming and his tail swishing against the porch floorboards.

"Punkin! Am I glad to see you, Boy!" Braedon knelt down on the porch and threw his arms around the dog's neck. "I've missed you, Buddy! Did you sense that, Boy?" After the two of them wallowed around for a while, he finally rose. "Come on, eat supper with us. Then I'll take you home so Charity and Adrianna won't stay up all night worrying about you."

Charity sneaked to both the front and back doors from time to time when Adrianna would be watching a TV program. She noticed her daughter's attention would sometimes stray from the set when the girl gazed out one of the windows in the back family room. On the way from the TV room through the French doors leading to the breakfast nook, they bumped into each other. Apparently, they both were secretly planning to look out the back door for the umpteenth time. The ring of the doorbell startled them both.

When Charity had made her way through the house and opened the front door, there stood Braedon with Punkin, both of them looking rather sheepish. She let out an audible sigh. "There you are, Boy! Finally!"

Adrianna came running through the house. "Where have you been, Punkin?"

"He landed on my front porch this evening. I'm sorry, I didn't have the heart to bring him home right away. As a matter of fact, he ate beef-vegetable stew with me. Hope you don't mind," Braedon apologized.

"You've been missing him around that house, haven't you, Bray?" Charity asked.

"Yeah, I sure have been missing him," he confessed.

"Guess we can look forward to more of his impulsive behavior," she remarked.

"Yeah, and if I'm lucky, I can look forward to more unexpected visits," Braedon reached down and patted Punkin's head.

"Where's Willow?" Adrianna wanted to know.

"Waiting in the truck. I've got to hurry home and get her in bed." He motioned toward the truck and then turned back around as a thought occurred to him. "Hey, could you two tear yourselves away from boxing things up to make a trip to the Grave Creek Mound tomorrow?"

"Yeah, we can tear ourselves away! Can't we, Mom?" Adrianna answered.

Charity grinned. "Yes, I guess we can tear ourselves away for a day or so. It's time I start doing some real work on this project."

"Would you like me to drive my truck, or do you want to drive your van?" he asked.

"Let's just take my van, Bray."

"K. See you in the morning, Charlie!"

"See ya."

Charity wakened, wrapped in a cocoon of quilts, wishing she could save the article she had been writing in her dreams. Stretching across the bed, she reached for her pad and pen to jot down notes from the logical parts she remembered. Reminding herself that she was going to view the Grave Creek Mound and visit the complex there, she practically floated down the stairs, through the living room, dining room, and into the kitchen in her white gown and robe to make coffee. The sun streamed through the windows; as she stood at the sink filling up the container with water to pour into the pot, she noticed the brilliant yellow of the large forsythia bush at the side of the yard. She smiled to herself, thinking how much her mother must have enjoyed the view.

She turned around, looking over the room as if through Alice's eyes. The Fostoria glassware on the glass shelves above a corner counter sparkled in the light from a nearby window. Cream-colored and rose pink tie-back curtains further brightened up the Shasta-yellow walls. It dawned on her that the colors in both the kitchen and the breakfast nook with its white French doors leading into the family room gave an illusion of bright and pretty flower gardens. Having poured her coffee into a lovely blue cup and placed a slice of buttered toast on its small matching saucer, she went out onto the front porch. A pleasant breeze softly stroked her face as she sat down in a rocker. While she sipped the coffee and rocked back and forth, she watched the leaves at the top of tall trees as they jostled against each other. She searched the blue sky for clouds wondering if the soft rustling was a portent of rain, and then dismissed the thought at the sight of the wisps of white clouds drifting over them. Gratitude to God rose from the depths of her being, and she longed to have her Bible or a devotional to read.

A sleepy-headed, disheveled Adrianna, in a floral pajama-short set, opened the door a crack and stood gazing out at the wildflowers waving in a field. "Think it's going to rain?" she asked.

"No, but I wondered that myself when I saw the leaves moving back and forth," Charity answered, glancing toward the trees. Turning her head, she eyed her daughter and spoke tenderly. "Honey, go fix your cereal and bring it out here to eat. It's such a nice morning to eat breakfast outside. Oh, before you go to the kitchen, would you hand me my Bible from the coffee table?"

When Adrianna handed her the Bible, she turned to Psalm 23 and read it aloud even though she had known it by heart since childhood. She wanted to see it on the page and consider each line as she voiced her own thoughts. *The Lord is my shepherd, and I need Him to shepherd me, to show me the way I should walk, to lead me into paths of righteousness for His name's sake.*

Before getting dressed, she called Cassie to see if she wanted to accompany them to the mound. "Sure, especially if Bray is going to take photos," Cassie said.

"Well, no, I've asked him to wait until we do the research and interviews before he takes his photos." Charity didn't think she needed to explain.

"Do you know what you are asking of him? It's sort of like asking him, please don't breathe until I say all clear! Besides, don't you think he should take pictures or videos when you are interviewing people?"

Charity thought about it for a few seconds before answering, "I think that would work."

"I'll phone Zak. He'll want in on this trip."

"Fine. Could you guys make it here in an hour?"

"Consider us on our way there!"

With the women dressed in their agreed-upon casual khaki shorts and blue tunic tees and the men wearing denim shirts and jeans to easily spot each other if separated, they looked like a team as they piled into the minivan. The young girls wore their usual colorful capri sets, also planned.

"Oh, wait, I have to put Punkin in the house." Charity swung the passenger door open.

"I wouldn't do that," Zak said. "As long as we might be gone, he may have to go outside before you return."

Charity didn't feel good about leaving him out again, but she thought their friend was right. If they were gone for hours, it could get uncomfortable for the dog. She ran back into the house for a container of dog food and a bowl of water. Punkin sat down on the porch when she told him to stay; and she saw he was still watching as Braedon drove the van across the paved strip where the wooden bridge had once stood, and her heart caught with love for him.

It was a very noisy trip with the adults discussing the information Charity had already uncovered about the South Charleston Mound, the Grave Creek Mound, and the center for research. When they grew quiet for a little while, each absorbed in their own thoughts, the girls started singing, "Row, row, row your boat." They stopped only once to use restrooms, pump gas, and purchase hotdogs which they ate in the van, sipping from the cans of soda Braedon had brought in a cooler.

Driving around the streets of Moundsville, they were struck with awe at the sight of the Grave Creek Mound. Once parked, Charity suggested they walk around the streets to get the feel of the town. Zachary rolled his eyes, but the others were enthusiastic. As they approached the mound, they looked for Dr. Joseph, who had declined an appointment at his home in Charleston in favor of meeting Charity at the mound. They stared at the largest Adena mound in the state and one of the tallest ever constructed. Its top rose sixty-five feet, and the team had already discussed the fact that it had been nearly seventy feet originally. From a distance, beyond the black iron fencing, Dr. Joseph looked like a miniature figure in a blue polo shirt and dark dress slacks as he stood at the base, looking up toward the top.

To gain access, they had to enter the Grave Creek Mound Archae-ological Complex and walk past the gift shop to the end of the hall, where glass double doors opened to a rest area with tables and chairs. There they found steps leading up to the grounds surrounding the ancient burial site.

"Oh my..." Charity was the one to speak first. "The enormity of this mound is far more impressive in person than mere pictures can depict."

"That depends on the photograph," Braedon informed her. Over-hearing their remarks as they drew nearer, Dr. Joseph agreed. "Yes, no matter how many times I've been here, I'm always amazed by the height and width of this mound. Do you know that this huge mound held only three people? In parts of Ohio and Pennsylvania, one mound alone could contain twenty, thirty, and even sixty large skeletons."

Braedon hurriedly slipped his backpack off. Unzipping one of the compartments, he handed Charity her notebook and pen. She began scribbling notes as quickly as possible, questions already formulating in her mind, and he adjusted the video camera. However, they soon learned that Dr. Joseph did not want to treat this visit as a lecture in a classroom or a regular interview. His sixty-five-year-old physical frame was relaxed, and he leisurely rubbed his gray mustache as he gazed at the magnificent earthwork before him. A lock of gray hair fell onto his forehead, shadowing his fading brown eyes. His tone as he talked was conversational. Spreading his arms as if he were about to fly away in a moment of wonder, he said, "This extraordinary conical burial mound is two hundred ninety-five feet in diameter. Originally, a five-foot moat surrounded the base. It's a shame that its sixty-nine, nearly seventy feet height was leveled down to sixty-five. It seems like a desecration when you consider the ceremonies that must have taken place during the times of interments." He pointed to the top. "Why, there was once even a saloon allowed to set atop."

"It's hard to believe that people would frequent a place there!" Cassie interrupted. "Can you imagine coming out of that building at night and meandering down the side of something this tall?"

"More to the point," Dr. Joseph replied, "Can you imagine the foolishness of leveling a mound and placing a business on top of something of such significant historical importance, not to mention the disrespect of a burial place?" They could only nod their heads in agreement at the serious, dark look he gave them. As they followed around to the south side of the mound, he pointed out the old well house and museum building now in disrepair. On rounding the southwest corner, a stone wall rose up with the fence on the street side of the mound. At the northwest corner, he stopped and informed them with gravity lowering his voice, "This is where they first dug into the mound."

"They?" Charity examined the disapproval displayed on his face.

"Local amateurs in 1858. I'll e-mail you the information about the tunnels, which probably destroyed important data that could have been compared to other mounds." Having replied, his upper teeth bit down softly into his lower lip before he added, "A lot of looters came through after that." Bringing himself out of his bleak reverie, he continued. "You'll see some interesting exhibits and information in the Archeological Complex in a little while, but most artifacts found in the mounds throughout the country ended up at the Smithsonian."

"Wasn't there a sandstone tablet with some type of inscription found inside one of the two rooms discovered in the center of the mound?" Charity asked.

"I see you've been doing your homework, dear girl. Yes, it was purportedly found among broken pottery and other stones in the top chamber by one person, but then another man said that was not so, that he had found it while carrying dirt out of the mound. There was a great deal of excitement and controversy at the time until someone revealed through an 1800 book all the mistakes of characters when compared to previously viewed unknown symbols on ancient tablets and the walls of caves." With that, he straightened up. "Well, let's climb those steps so you can have a good view from the top."

Repositioning his backpack and the video camera, Braedon followed behind Dr. Joseph. Charity, Adrianna, and Willow fell next in line, with Cassie and Zak bringing up the rear. Even with the soles of their walking shoes, their feet made scuffling sounds on each of the solid stone steps. Looking down as they neared, the top of the walkway appeared very narrow. Once at the top, everyone took a deep breath. A stone wall encircled the open area, and the professor said he figured it was about sixty feet in circumference. In the center stood a monument, which looked like an obelisk bearing the date 1942. Letters carved on all four sides were directional indicators: N for north, S for south, W for west, and E for east. The group stood looking out over the town and the mountains surrounding the closed but still formidable looking West Virginia Moundsville Penitentiary, with its architectural design looking every inch like a turreted castle; its 1866 gothic structure spreading out for blocks.

When curiosity drew them like a magnet back into the Grave Creek Mound Archeological Complex, the museum and research center, where they were privileged to view artifacts from various regional locations, Braedon lingered behind. "I'll be inside in a few," he said. Willow and Adrianna giggled as they skipped to catch up with the group.

All of them felt thrilled at the sight of the exhibits displayed in the museum. A huge full-bodied Stegodon zdanskyi "Roofed Tooth" skeleton and large mammoth skulls greeted them. Charity was thrilled when Dr. Joseph pointed out some prehistoric artifacts in glass cases positioned on the wide open floor space and others enclosed on the walls downstairs and upstairs. He explained that he believed the museum switched some displays every so often. The tube pipes, pipes with various animal effigies, and sandstone gorgets excited her. She could tell Zak was highly interested in the stone tools such as pestles and axes. Cassie was mesmerized by the pottery and the clay, bead, bone, and shell necklaces displayed beside the tooth pendants.

After quite some time had passed, Charity wanted to share what she had already seen and read with Braedon. She went in search of him. Stepping out of the complex and walking a few steps, she spotted him squatting next to the iron fence with a new camera pointed toward the top of the mound. She noticed he had purchased other equipment, too, some of which she couldn't guess their function, but they sat on a mat spread near where he hunkered down. For a moment, she stood with her hands on her hips. Striding across the expanse between the complex and the mound, she cleared her throat. She noted that he turned slowly, fidgeting with the lens, giving himself a chance to mentally compose something to say to her. Obviously, nothing but the truth would come to mind. After all, how could he explain the large backpack open at his feet, which she had assumed contained notebooks, snacks, and treats, and the camera now hanging from his neck? Though the tripod wasn't as yet extended, one leg was looped into the backpack's strap. No, the evidence was stacked against him.

"I'm sorry, Charlie. I-"

"No, you're not, Bray. You're practically giddy with purpose."

He tilted his head and tightened his lips in a lopsided grin of admission.

"Well, come on into the center, and look at some of these artifacts with me. If they allow you to take photos and video, please do, so we can go over the pictures when we lay all the information out."

CHAPTER 8

Relief flooded Braedon's mind and poured over his posture as he closed his backpack, heaved it onto his back, and followed Charity into the museum. As he adjusted his lens to zoom onto the stone tools and animal effigies, he was unexpectedly distracted by a familiar male figure in navy work clothes looking intently at a display of granite and banded slate arrowheads. "Roy?"

The man refocused his vision and attention on Braedon. "Oh, hello, Braedon. Jus' killin' time with my nephew, Henry, while I'm waitin' to finish up some business here in Moundsville." He pointed toward the young man in a black t-shirt and jeans who lowered the bill of his ball cap, nodded in Braedon's direction, and then turned away to look at more arrowheads. "And you?"

"Seeing the sights. Small world, eh?"

"Yeah. You're taking photos, too. Aren't you?"

"That's me. I take pics of everything everywhere I go."

"So you do. Ever since Vera gave you your first camera."

"That's right."

"Is Charity with you?"

"Yes, and Cassie and Zak, too."

"Well, well. Makin' a day of it, I guess."

"Yes, enjoying a road trip and stopping off to see some of the parks," Braedon, feeling something was off with Roy and his nephew – but not sure what – replied. He deliberately focused on a marvelously detailed turtle through the lens of his camera.

"Hey, Roy." Charity approached the man, taking note that he was the one who seemed uncomfortable this time. "Isn't it something that we are all from Country Lanes and run into each other here, of all places?"

"Yeah. Like Braedon jus' said, it's a small world."

Braedon quickly lowered his camera from his face and turned toward her. "Yes, I was just telling Roy we're enjoying a road trip and stopping off at some of the parks."

She looked across at her childhood friend and saw the old, shared-secret expression in his knowing look. Smiling, she nodded, "Yes, it's great to get away from the house and all the packing we have to do and just see other sights."

Roy nodded, too. "Yeah, you probably need a break by now." He looked around with a confused demeanor. "But it's odd you would end up here at the Grave Creek Mound and the museum."

"Odd?" She raised her eyebrows.

He seemed to come back from wherever his mind had taken him. "Oh, maybe odd is not the word to use. It jus' seems like more than a coincidence." He gave her a curious look.

It was Charity's turn to feel confused by his words. "It does?"

He laughed like his old, relaxed self. "I'm so tired of drivin' and takin' care of business, I'm not makin' a whole lotta sense. I hope I can wind this business up soon and get home in one piece."

Since he seemed more like the old Roy who had been her parents' long-time friend, she shrugged off the questions beginning to form in her mind and relaxed. "Well, I hope you have a safe trip back home. Stop and pick up coffee, and be careful."

He grinned and winked at her. "That I will do, young lady. You guys be careful, too." As Cassie made her way over to them, he put up a hand to wave. "See y'all later."

When Braedon began to position himself and focus his camera again, Charity couldn't resist asking, "Why didn't you tell Roy what we were actually doing here?"

"I don't really know. A gut feeling, I think. He seemed a little too surprised and uncomfortable at running into us here."

"Oh, he probably was just surprised to run into anyone from Country Lanes. It just happened to be us."

"Hmm... I'm not so sure. Surprised, yes, but once he heard an explanation, why would he act like our presence made him uncomfortable? Can't help but wonder about his real reason for coming here."

"He said he was taking care of business. You're not suggesting he followed us here, are you?"

"No. He was in the building before we walked inside. But, I'm wondering what kind of business he does have in this area."

"You know Roy. He would tell you that whatever business he has here is none of *your* business."

"Well, thank you, Charlie, for being his spokesperson! That put me in my place!" They both laughed and continued perusing the various artifacts.

After thanking and saying goodbye to Dr. Joseph, they made plans to stop at a fast food place on the way home.

CHAPTER 9

The next morning, while she sipped her coffee on the porch, Charity chatted with Cassie on her cell phone. The two of them agreed to spend the afternoon and evening laying out the index cards, sticky notes, and notebook pages to make an outline for the article and decide what angle they would use. She was glad she had showered and slipped on fresh jeans and a faded blue t-shirt when Braedon pulled up in his truck just as she ended her conversation.

"Good Morning, Ms. Charity! Have you recovered from our adventure into the ancient past?"

"Actually, I think it's still with me. I can't wait until Cassie and I lay out all the notes again from our research, and now, from each of the mound visits."

"Whoa now, lady. Don't you want to take in more sights and question a lot more people who are knowledgeable in the archaeological field?"

"Yes, I *do*, but right now, I want to gather the information and determine what direction we are taking before I ask those questions."

"Does this mean you will need my photos to complete your directional map?"

"No, I don't think so. You have more pictures to take of the sites we've already visited."

"Thanks to you." His handsome jaw jutted out as he tilted his head back and squared his shoulders.

She couldn't help taking in his broad shoulders and chest in his white T-shirt and the stance of his strong denim-clad legs.

Her scrutiny did not go unnoticed by him, and he grinned until she rose out of the rocker. "I'll see if Adrianna is dressed and ready to take a walk over the property. I want to describe what each section looked like while I was growing up before businesses changed the surrounding landscape."

"Mind if I walk with you? Your memories are mine, you know."

She smiled tenderly at his statement of truth. "Yeah, I know. Maybe you can recall a few things I may forget to tell her."

He called Willow's name toward the truck, and his daughter jumped out, happiness written across her features as she smoothed her lilac tank top over blue capris.

As the four of them strolled along the border of the property where a covered bridge and a dirt road had once led to an intersection in Country Lanes, Punkin started switching his tail from side to side and running with glee toward a tan, bare-chested boy in jeans cut off just above the knee heading their way. The new arrival's tawny head and amber eyes glowed with affection while the dog and boy romped around before coming close to them. Obviously, Punkin had found a new playmate while Charity was gone and her mother was still alive.

Adrianna's eyes lit up as she quickly tried to straighten her pink sleeveless blouse and capris. "Hi!"

"Hi, yourself!" The boy smiled, showing white teeth and healthy gums, a smile a person would want to see often.

"I'm Adrianna, and this is my mom, Charity, and our friends Braedon and Willow."

"Hey, you're Mrs. Payne's granddaughter! She talked a lot about your mom and you." When everyone waited expectantly, he quickly added, "I'm the Gordon's grandson, Nick. I spend most of my summers here. But I think my mom and dad want to move in with my grandma now that she's all alone."

"How old are you?" Adrianna asked.

"Ten and a half, goin' on eleven," he proudly answered, but looked a little embarrassed when they all noticed a gun stuck in the band of his jeans.

"Is that thing real? It looks real." Willow's curiosity overcame her politeness.

Cheeks flushing red, the young boy pulled the toy out of his shorts. "Nah... it's a toy."

"A *vintage* toy," Braedon emphasized. "The gun doesn't have the red plastic in the barrel."

Nick pointed out the exposed opening in the barrel. "Yeah, I found it in my grandpa's attic. The red plastic is a dead giveaway that a gun is only a toy now." He seemed to feel better about carrying it in their presence when Adrianna examined it and uttered the word *cool*.

Charity smiled a big welcome. "Well, Nick, grandson of the Gordons, would you like to join us as we walk the perimeters of the property? I remember when it looked a lot different."

With Adrianna and Willow nodding at him, he grinned readily and said, "Yeah, sure." Focusing his attention on Charity in interest, he asked, "How different?"

"Well, for starters, right over there where that car dealership parking lot ends and a newly paved road begins, a creek flowed so deeply that we had to have a covered bridge in order to cross it."

"That's why the pavement shows wide cracks and often must be repaired," Braedon added. "We kids used to play in it and catch bait for fishing."

"Now I do," Nick stated.

"What do you mean?" Charity stopped and fixed her eyes on the boy's face.

"That stream runs under all this," he said as he slid his outstretched arms back and forth. "It runs under the pavement and new roads before it turns a bit and comes out further on down at the far end of your land." He was obviously impressed with the impact his simple statement made on his hearers. "That's how I met your mom, ma'am. I was explorin' and ran across the creek where I could catch bait to fish with my grandpa, and she and your dog were sittin' above the bank lookin' at the water." Now he appeared even more impressed with himself as he saw the man and woman exchange surprised glances. "Do ya'll want me to show you where it opens up?" He wore an amused grin as the couple looked directly at him and nodded in speechless agreement.

Walking a distance through high grass and wildflowers before scrambling down an embankment where the land leveled off at the southwestern end of the property line, they saw the creek running as full and smooth as it ever had in the past.

Pointing to a large boulder protruding from the opposite hillside, Nick told them, "That's where I saw your mom sittin' the first day I came down here."

Charity envisioned Alice sitting in jeans and the checkered flannel shirt she liked to wear, swinging her booted legs over the edge of the large rock to watch the clear water flow over pebbles in the creek. A refreshing sense of peace washed over her. It would be just like her mother to sit there and talk to the Creator of all life. Her daughter now gazed at the water rippling around the stones in the creek bed.

"Can Willow and I wade in the water, Mommy?" Adrianna's voice brought her mother back to the present.

"Sure, Honey, kick off your shoes and jump in!"

As the couple watched the girls wading through the water and Nick searching along the banks for signs of crawfish and frogs, they were both reminded of two other young girls and a boy and smiled at each other. Stepping gingerly on rocks jutting out of the water, they took seats on the boulder. After sitting there feeling the peace of the place for a while, Charity began to look around at the layout of the land, spotting holes dug on the hill above where they sat.

"Hey, Nick, do you know anything about those holes up there?"

The boy stopped and straightened up, looking in the direction she indicated with her head. "Beats me. I sure didn't dig 'em."

"Did you see anybody around whenever you were here scooping bait?"

"Nah... I think I would've noticed too...'specially if they were dig-gin' holes."

"Maybe it's some kind of animal digging the holes, Charlie," Brae-don suggested.

She considered this theory for a moment. "Yeah, I guess so. Even Punkin likes to dig after something." Holding onto trees, she hoisted herself closer to one of the openings and put her hands on her hips. "Still, these holes are awfully wide and deep," she said in a puzzled tone.

Braedon drew closer with a frown. "So they are. Hmm..." He stooped and peered into the opening and then moved to another one and did the same. "Doesn't look like anything is in them or ever has been. Maybe some animal got carried away with his clawing...."

"Maybe…" Charity decided to dismiss the questions since there was no explanation.

Once back at the house, they all ate sandwiches and drank iced tea on the porch, the couple relaxing at the table and the girls and their new friend on the floor at the other end. Every once in a while, laughter burst from the kids' direction, causing Charity and Braedon to smile again as they, without saying a word, shared fond memories.

"Wow," Charity spoke out loud. "This has been fun, but it's time I get things ready for Cassie and me to lay out the material in some kind of order."

"Okay, but could I ask one favor of you?" Braedon's eyes wore a pretentious pleading expression.

"You can ask," she teased.

"May I take Punkin home with me? Just for the night?"

She tilted her head with her lips pressed together the way she always did when she understood her friend Bray's true feelings. "Yes, Bray Buddy, you may take him home with you for one night."

"Then, I best be going since those clouds rolling in look a bit ominous. Nick, you want a ride before that cloud bursts?"

Jumping up from his seat on the porch floor, the boy looked up at the sky. "Sure thing, Mr. Moore!"

While she and Charity were picking up the plates and glasses on the porch when their company had left, Adrianna discovered Nick, anxious for a ride home, had accidentally left his toy gun. "Mom, look, Nick's gun!"

"Oh, he was in such a hurry! No problem, we can drop it off tomorrow. He surely won't need it until then. Just set it on the round table near the door in the sunroom, so we don't forget it."

By the time Cassie drove up to the house, thunder rumbled in the distance. She called out the driver's window to Charity, who stood on the porch. "I can't believe I made it before the storm! We're bound to get a downpour!"

"I thought you'd changed your mind," Charity yelled back.

"Nope, just running a tad behind."

"Well, why don't you pull your car into the garage where it will stay dry and be closer to the side door?"

"What about your car?"

"It'll be all right. I don't plan to go anywhere tonight."

Once inside, Charity steered her friend to the dining room, where she had rolled a cart with a coffee pot, cups, spoons, powdered creamer, sugar, and snack crackers. The table held a box with the printed material they would need to lay out on it. "When we have gone through these notes and laid them out in a particular arrangement, I'm going to leave them like that so we can enter them into the computer in proper order."

"Great. Let's get started!" Cassie's enthusiasm showed.

Charity suddenly felt blessed to have a friend like Cassie, who had always been ready to chip in, not out of duty or obligation to their friendship, but because she was able to catch the spark of interest in whatever project her childhood playmate began and share the same wavelength. They each pulled out a chair, and sorting through the pile, they started grouping the papers according to similar information, like children playing a matching game.

After some time, the mother instinct took over, and Charity went upstairs to check on her daughter. Finding Adrianna asleep in bed with a book on top of the covers, she carefully inserted the bookmark between the pages, placed the book on the nightstand, slipped the quilt at the foot of the bed over her daughter, and clicked off the lamp. As thunder boomed overhead, she wondered if it would wake her little sleeping beauty.

When she returned to the dining room, Cassie was busy stirring creamer and sugar into her second cup of coffee. Charity poured coffee and creamer into her own second cup, suddenly aware of the flickering lights. "I have an idea, Cassie."

"Oh no, not another idea. Let's finish this one first."

"Okay, Zak Collins."

"Oh oh... did I come across *that* bad?"

Charity laughed and nodded. "Almost."

"Okay, what's your idea?"

"Since it's a stormy evening, why don't you stay overnight?"

"That's your idea?"

"That's my question."

"We haven't had a sleepover in years, Charity!"

"I know. You can borrow a pair of my PJs and sleep in the small guest room between Adrianna's room and mine since we're all grown up now."

They both felt like kids again, like the years had slipped back in time.

Lightning lit up the room even as the lamp over the table was dimming and flickering continuously. Charity remembered to go to the kitchen and pull out a black flashlight her mother always kept in the drawer nearest the side window. She also, as a precaution, lit a couple of oil lamps and set them upon the upper shelves in the dining room and candles on the table. Just as she picked up her cup again, the two women heard a clanging at the back door. Startled, they looked at each other questioningly. By the time they were ready to dismiss the sound from their minds as wind pushing against the screen door, a louder metallic scraping accompanied the strong turning of the knob.

"Someone is trying to unlock the back door," Charity whispered as Cassie nodded. It took a few moments of freezing upon hearing that eerie sound to decide to take action before it had a chance to escalate. Moving quickly into the breakfast nook with Cassie right on her heels, she approached the back door.

"Who is it?" She demanded, but no one answered.

"I said, *who are you?*" Still, no answer. Just as she thought the intruder must have gone away, loud banging made her and Cassie jump at the same time. It became clear to both women that someone had gone from pounding with their fists to forcing his shoulder against the door. Charity caught Cassie around the waist just as she paled and looked like she was going to faint.

Adrianna's soft voice broke through the terror building up inside them. "What's going on, Mommy?"

Oh, Lord, what do I do? Help me make the right decision, the mother in her prayed.

"Come into the living room," she instructed in a whisper to Cassie and Adrianna. Once there, she tried the landline only to find it dead. *Is it dead because of the storm, or did someone cut the line?* Keeping such dreadful thoughts to herself, she grabbed her cell phone from the round table in the sunroom and clicked on Braedon's number.

He answered in a sleepy voice. "Hello."

"Bray, it's Charity. Someone's trying to break into the house!"

"What did you say?"

"Someone is breaking into my house!"

"Hide, Charlie, and I'll be right there!"

Almost in a trance-like state, she started to place the phone back on the table when she saw Nick's toy gun in the sunroom. An idea popped into her head. *What if it doesn't work, Charity? What then?* Seeing the two in the living room huddled together, she motioned them to the large sunroom closet, gesturing with her hands that they were to hide in the back behind all the coats and jackets. Having done that, she took the gun into the living room, and though the rough pushing against the door suddenly changed to wood splintering by some hard object, she steeled herself for what she planned to do.

Running to the back door, she swiped the curtain back from the high window and held the gun up, so it was visible to the intruder. "Come on in, you coward. I'm ready!!"

The screen door slammed shut, almost making her lose her nerve until she heard footsteps hitting mud puddles as the person ran away. A distant growl and snarl with an abrupt yelp pierced through the rumbles of thunder on their way to her eardrums. *Did he run into something?*

As she walked stealthily, she tried to catch any outside sounds. What if he had tried to break through any of these windows? Why didn't he? Was he afraid of cutting himself? Could the answer really be that simple? She hesitated before opening the closet until the gleam of headlights from Braedon's truck slid over the sunroom. Not waiting for him to ring the bell or knock, she swung open the door.

"I called the authorities," he announced as he came barreling inside, rifle in hand and slicker wide open. "I was heading around back when I saw your silhouette through the sunroom sheers."

At the familiar sound of Braedon's voice, Cassie and Adrianna worked their way out of the closet but continued to stand close together.

"I didn't even think of that. Sorry, Bray, you were closer, and I didn't consider I was putting you in danger. He's gone now anyway."

"That's okay. I'm *glad* you called!"

Motioning toward the rifle, she asked, "Were you going to *shoot* him?"

"No. I hoped to hold him off until the police could get here."

"I couldn't shoot anyone," she confessed.

"Not with that thing, you wouldn't!" He pointed out as she became aware she was still holding the toy gun and grinned.

"Well, thank God it worked!" she exclaimed.

"We need to install an alarm and cameras here, Charlie." Before she could voice the protest on the tip of her tongue, he added, "For Adrianna's sake."

Hearing the last phrase, she could only nod in agreement.

His expression of relief suddenly changed to one of concern again. "Have you seen Punkin?"

"No. He's with you, isn't he?"

"Not now. I guess I was acting strangely after your call, rushing around and everything. He probably heard your voice. I wanted him to stay with Willow and Livie since they were asleep upstairs, but when I jumped into the truck and started the engine, he jumped in the back. When we were almost here, he jumped out and took off at a run."

"Oh no, Bray. He may have followed that man. And your poor girls... you'd better go home to them now. The authorities will be here, and they can take a look around." Just as she said that, headlights lit up the porch.

"Okay, Willow and I will be over first thing in the morning. Don't think I'll get any sleep, though, until I know Punkin is home with one of us."

"Same here."

It was useless for the police officers to try to track footprints since the rain obscured them. All they could do was take pictures of the scrapes and cuts on the back door and write a report of the incident.

No one slept well that night, dressed in their clothes. Every small sound caused eyelids to flutter. When Charity woke, surprised that she had slept at all, she heard someone outside moving along the side of the house and around toward the porch. Opening the door as quietly as she could, she took a cautious step while keeping a hand on the doorknob. She gasped at the sight of Braedon carrying Punkin in both arms.

"Taking him to the vet, Charlie. Found him beyond the barn. Looks like someone hit him on top of the head with an ax."

"Oh, Punkin!" She cried as she ran to them, but Punkin was unresponsive. "Let me go with you, Bray!" She raced inside and up the stairs as fast as her legs would go to tell Cassie where she was going and ask her to stay with Adrianna and Willow.

Both Charity and Braedon were relieved when the vet said that it was only a glancing blow and had merely sliced off the skin and fur between the dog's ears, just enough of an impact to knock him out. A dazed Punkin finally came around while the doctor treated the wound. He gave them an antiseptic powder to put on the wound twice daily.

Charity watched day after day as Braedon sat on the top step of the porch applying the medicated powder to Punkin's head wound. She couldn't help but notice the man's gentle and affectionate attitude as the dog sat trustingly beside him. Once the wound was dressed, Punkin would turn his head and look up into Braedon's face with undeniable love in his brown eyes. One day, while watching this interaction between man and dog, her heart filled with warmth and her eyes with unshed tears, and both would have overflowed in an embarrassing display of emotion had she not stood up to pour iced tea into glasses.

After cleansing his hands with sanitizer and inspecting his white tee-shirt for traces of the powder, Braedon rose to take the glass she offered. Their fingers touched, and he looked at her in surprise when she quickly wiped her hand on her denim outfit and turned away as she began talking about the weather. He stared at her silently until she turned back around and gazed at him. He then saw the blush spreading across her cheeks. He couldn't help but grin and relax when he realized she was flustered.

"Punkin's wound is healing nicely," he said in an attempt to put her at ease.

"That's good. That's good," she responded. "You're great with him."

"He's family."

She raised her eyebrows.

"I can't help feeling like he's part of our family, too, Charlie."

The blush fading, her blue eyes held understanding as she nodded.

For a few minutes, his face took on an earnest expression as if he wanted to say something, but he lifted the glass to his lips and drank slowly instead.

As Braedon drove away, Charity and Punkin stood on the porch watching his truck until it was out of sight. "Well, Boy, we both have to figure out what to do about the affection we feel toward that man. As for me, I can't let it grow. In time I have to return to my life."

Punkin cocked his head as if to say, "What life?" Or was she reading her own thought into his pose, she wondered.

CHAPTER 10

After Braedon and Zachary installed alarms and cameras at both the front and back of the house, Charity worked with Cassie every day for a while with greater ease, transferring information into the computer setting on the dining room table. She couldn't help noticing how quickly her friend's fingers swept across the keyboard. She, herself, typed well but cautiously to catch mistakes or oversights. A person would think that since she wrote articles for a living, she would type pretty fast. She was better with a pencil or pen and research. Besides, she was a stickler for accuracy, sometimes changing her mind about the order of material or inclusion of new material as she saw the information in print. Once they had entered all the information, she decided she wanted Braedon's pictures included after all. Later, they could select the best photos for the article.

"Hey, Bray, are you free to bring your pictures over to include them with our research this morning? Cassie has a printer and scanner we can set up."

"Oh, you want my pictures now, do you?"

"Yes, I do!"

"Well, it's a good thing Zak and I sneaked off to buy new equipment and take photos of each mound we've seen so far. In some cases, I turned his back to the camera to help the viewer imagine the height and width of each of the burial sites."

"Hmm…" Her voice lowered in mock dismay. " Okay…I'm inclined to forgive you at this point."

"That's generous of you, Charlie."

"Think nothing of it, Bray. We now have a work in progress!"

"But can you and Adrianna meet the three of us at the CL restaurant for a meal first?"

"The three of you?"

"Willow, Livie, and me."

"Well, yeah! Finally, I get to actually see Livie! You bet!" She paused as she re-evaluated her appearance. "Give me a few minutes to tidy up, and then we'll meet you guys there. Okay?"

"Sure. We all could use this break. See you gals there."

Dressed in a fresh blue floral blouse and jeans, Charity was in a happy mood when she and Adrianna slid into their seats at the table where Braedon, Willow, and Olivia waited. Olivia's cheeks beamed dimples across the table. She looked cool in her white tank top and mid-thigh denim shorts. "Wow, Charity, you look even more beautiful than I remembered! Don't you think, Bray?"

Taken off guard and unexpectedly embarrassed, he opened his mouth, but no sound came.

Sensing it was an awkward moment for him, Charity came to his rescue. She leaned her head over the table. "And you have matured from a cute teenager into a lovely young woman while I've been gone, Livie!".

Braedon sat back, obviously relieved and grateful for the interruption. "So, is everyone hungry?"

A low, sultry voice answered. "Well, I hope so. Here's your menu, Braedon." Luna Brecknor stood smiling down at him. As she smiled dreamily into his eyes, she loosened the hairband and let the luxurious brown waves cascade over one shoulder. She finally forced herself to turn her gray-green sight from him long enough to hand out the menus. "Oh, hello, Olivia. You must be home on break."

Irritated by the girl fawning over her brother, Olivia began, "Yeah, hello, Loon...n...." Braedon shot his sister a sharp glance before she continued, "*Luna*. I guess you work here now."

"Some of us have to work our way through college." Everyone except the girls knew she referred to Vera's life savings her daughter had inherited.

Charity coughed softly. "That's commendable, Luna."

Luna glared at Charity as if her very presence in the restaurant insulted her.

Braedon cleared his throat. "What is your major?"

"Business. So I can help Dad with the hardware store someday. I work there part-time, too."

He nodded, considering the feasibility of her goal.

She grinned as if they shared a secret. "But what I really want to do is marry a nice man and mother his children." She gave him a knowing look and winked.

"Uh...I see... we'd better order some lunch before my stomach starts growling out loud."

"Sure thing." She drew a notepad and pen out of her white apron pocket to jot down their orders.

When the slim waitress walked away with a slinky sway of hips under her clinging pale-green summer dress, Willow eyed Adrianna. She dunked her index finger inside her mouth, pretending to silently gag, but stopped when her father sent a hiss her way. The girls burst into giggles despite his warning.

Luna brought the servings quickly and efficiently when a couple took a table in her section. The food was delicious and one of the main topics of their relaxed conversation. When they had finished their meal, however, she approached their table again. "Will there be anything else I can get you? Dessert?" She gazed, once more, into Braedon's eyes.

Charity rose. "Thank you, Luna. Not for me, though. Adrianna and I have to get back to Punkin."

With a sneer, the waitress' head turned in her direction. "You still have that mangy old dog? He must be a hundred years old. I'd think he'd have crawled over the rainbow bridge a long time ago."

Charity's face heated up, and she stepped forward, ready to voice a nasty retort on her mind when Braedon jumped to his feet in an attempt at intervention. Brown eyes widening, he interjected loudly, "Oh, Okay, then. Thanks, Luna." He threw a large tip on the table she couldn't miss seeing. "See you around." The five of them hurried to the check-out counter near the door and made a speedy exit.

In anticipation of her two friends, and now teammates, on their way to work on the project, Charity hurried into the kitchen to brew coffee. When she turned on the water faucet, nothing happened. Disbelieving, she turned it off and on several times, opened the cabinet doors underneath the sink, and examined the water pipes, which looked perfectly normal.

She met Braedon at the front door with a look of consternation crossing her face.

"What's wrong, Charlie?"

"There's no running water this morning! I know I paid the bill!"

Braedon walked through the house and into the kitchen, where he, too, examined the pipes under the sink. "Pipes here look like they're intact, and there's no water standing from a leak. I'll go out and check the water pump. If it's okay, I'll crawl under the house to check for leaks."

It didn't take him long to check the water pump from the well hidden under the dome covering that looked like a big rock. She felt guilty knowing he would have to squeeze under the house. Maybe she wasn't as independent as she envisioned herself.

"I'm sorry to have to bother you, Bray. Wish this house had a basement."

"No bother, but I'll admit it won't be easy. And it will take time. Do you know where your mother kept wrenches?"

While Willow rocked on the front porch, waiting for Adrianna to wake up and come downstairs, Charity stood outside, off to the side of the kitchen, under the magnolia tree, watching Braedon slide under the house. As she handed him the tools and a large plastic bag on which he would lay, she felt terrible that she had to ask him to do this job since he came prepared to select and work his photos of the mounds into the assignment. At least he wore a black t-shirt and faded jeans instead of a dress shirt and slacks, she thought.

Finally emerging head first from the opening, he looked aggravated. He pulled the tools out and dusted dirt and webs from his clothes. "I hate to tell you this, Charlie, but the water was not turned off, and the pipes don't have a leak. It looks like someone has disconnected them in several places. There's water everywhere under there." He pointed to his damp and dirty clothes. "Good thing I had that bag to lie on."

"Wh...what?!"

"They've been disconnected."

"Who would do such a thing? Why? When?!"

"It's my guess," Braedon ventured, "someone who wants you to leave or give up the house. You didn't hear anything last night? What about Punkin?"

She looked away, trying to recall if she had heard anything unusual. "No. I was sound asleep upstairs last night and in the early morning hours. Punkin slept at the foot of Adrianna's bed."

"I can fix or replace the pipes, but it will take time out of our plans to buy them and do the work," he offered. "These pipes are pretty old."

"No. I'll call Carter the way Mom always did and ask him to fix or pick up new pipes and attach them. He could probably use the extra money and feel like he is doing her a favor. Just turn off the water completely."

Having called Carter, and then Cassie to ask her to bring coffee in a thermos and a couple of jugs of water, Charity handed the hand sanitizer to Braedon and grabbed a package of cinnamon rolls to heat in the microwave for a quick breakfast. Again, she gave permission for the girls to stay in the breakfast nook and play a board game Adrianna had found in one of the closets.

She and Braedon viewed the cameras' video, hoping to recognize the person who disconnected the water pipes. All they could make out was a person in a black jacket with the hood pulled up and his face down coming from the woods. As he approached the house, he veered to the side of the breakfast nook and kitchen. The camera didn't pick up his departure, which told them the culprit left from the side of the house and headed for the woods. It became evident to both of them that this perpetrator somehow knew cameras had been installed and where.

Officer Kerry Bertrand, who everyone he grew up around in Country Lanes persisted in calling Bert, slid out from underneath the house. Though somewhat still fit, his middle-aged frame struggled a bit to get up off the plastic trash bag Charity had given him. "It's a good thing you called me, Charity. Braedon's right. The pipes have been deliberately separated. Now, I need to see the video you mentioned." A younger officer handed him his hat as they stepped up onto the porch, waiting for her to take the lead.

In a few minutes, his blue eyes stared hard at the monitor's screen as he zoomed in and out on the figure in the dark hoodie. He smoothed his furrowed forehead and bushy gray brows with one hand. "There's something familiar about this person. But I can't put a finger on it. Can you print a picture out for me?"

It wasn't long before she handed him a couple of sheets bearing the culprit's image. "What I want to know is why anyone would want to do such a nasty thing to me?"

"That is my next question for you. This is getting serious, girl. After all, someone tried to break in here on that rainy night and ended up hurting your dog Punkin." He paused with a level look into her eyes. "Do you have any enemies or-"

Braedon's voice broke into the questioning. "No, she doesn't. Everyone around here loves this woman."

"*Or*," Bert continued with forced patience, "have you had any disagreements with anyone lately?"

Charity's blushing cheeks smiled. "I don't think I have any enemies." She searched her memory. "But I did have a slight disagreement with Roy. Other than that incident, I can't think of anything else. It wasn't anything but a spat, really."

Officer Bert waved the sheets in the air. "Well, this picture doesn't look like Roy. So, he's out. Plus, I don't believe he would ever sink that low to do something this nasty to you, Charity. Someone could have even hired a man to sneak and disconnect the pipes."

"But how would they know about the cameras and their location?"

"Stakeout. Could be." The officer looked through the dining room window. "Have you seen a suspicious vehicle parked near your property?"

"Not that I noticed. Of course, I wasn't looking for one, either."

Braedon interjected again, "I'm sure I would have noticed one on the road on my many trips over here."

The corner of Officer Bert's eyes crinkled. "Well, Lou, we'd better get back to the station with this report and pass these pictures around and see if anyone has any idea who this person is. Give us a call if you think of anything else, Charity."

"I will, Bert...*Officer* Bert. Thank you."

He motioned for the younger officer to follow him out.

Later, she and Braedon settled down at the dining room table with mugs, and the large thermos of coffee Cassie had brought with her. They began the work of laying out photos to select for the scanner set up on a nearby table.

"Oh, Bray! This is going to be a difficult job, selecting the best pictures. They are all good!" Charity exclaimed.

"Not really, Charlie. A few have too much light though I kept adjusting the camera as well as I could."

"You're the best judge of these photos, Bray. I don't see what we can contribute except scanning and inserting them," Cassie pointed out.

"Once I've picked several I think are good enough for the article, you, Zak, and Charlie can try to view them through the eyes of your readers," he replied. "There is one, though the angle is off and the lighting poor, you might find interesting, though."

He piqued their curiosity with his last statement, and they peered over the picture he placed before them.

Finally, Charity said, "I don't see anything different from what we saw at the Grave Creek Mound."

"I don't either, Bray," Cassie stated.

Braedon took the tip of a pen to point to a couple of men barely noticeable standing a few yards from the mound. Producing another picture of the outside of the museum, his pen pointed to the same two men off to the side of the building. "Now, look through this magnifying glass, girls, and tell me if you see anyone who looks familiar."

Again, the women peered as closely as they could before Charity asked, "Could these men be Roy and his nephew?"

"It sure looks like them," Cassie added.

"That's my guess," Braedon agreed.

"But Roy was already in the museum when we entered. Wasn't he?!" Charity exclaimed, pulling the photo closer.

"Maybe not," Braedon said. "He and his nephew could have been looking at the mound when we met Dr. Joseph and then tried to stay out of sight. Obviously, they were too curious about the artifacts to resist going into the museum. We were too busy viewing the items and listening to Dr. Joseph to notice when they came inside. With other people moving around, we weren't aware Roy was there until he stopped to look at the arrowheads, and you, too, stopped there."

"But why would he act surprised to see us?" Charity asked.

"Why, indeed?" he answered with the same question.

"Hey, guys! Give Roy a break! If we didn't notice him, he might not have noticed us!" Cassie threw her hands up.

"True," Braedon agreed. "Still, it appears he and his nephew are looking toward me."

"*Appears*, Braedon," Cassie emphasized. "But it doesn't mean he actually saw us."

At that, they all nodded and continued arranging the research and photos.

CHAPTER 11

I t had been years since the four friends sat dressed in blue jeans and t-shirts around the firepit in Charity's backyard. The new camping chairs were comfortable and secured their chilled cans of soda while they snacked on popcorn and roasted marshmallows. The temperature dropped a little when a cool breeze swept through the valley. An earlier meeting discussing relics found in the mounds having ended, the women spread light throws over their laps.

Adrianna, Willow, and their new friend, Nick, played spotlight at a little distance hiding behind trees and bushes. Olivia was monitoring the game. The hush reminded Charity of times she and her friends had played the game. It was a quiet game since no one wanted the light to expose their location. She glanced at Cassie and knew her friend remembered, too.

Punkin lay peacefully on the ground with his head resting on both front paws near Charity's legs.

She realized she hadn't felt this relaxed in a very long time. Watching the fire, encircled by large river rocks, shoot up flames as it crackled and popped put her in a mellow mood. She observed the glow on the faces of her friends as they stretched out their legs, obviously giving in to the relaxed atmosphere, too. She noticed Braedon gazing up at the full moon and couldn't help looking up to admire the night sky with its lovely display of stars. Lowering her vision again, her eyes met his in unspoken yet shared appreciation.

Cassie was the first to break the silence. "You know, we've been discussing the facts about the mounds and theories about the kind of relics stolen for some time now. But off the record, so to speak, there are a few strange beliefs I uncovered in my research."

"Oh?" Charity raised an eyebrow. "What do you mean by *strange*?"

Cassie pulled the rod holding her marshmallow away from the flames in order to see how well it had toasted. "Well, for one thing, there are theologians who believe the seven to ten-foot giants found in some of the mounds were offspring of fallen angels and the women they seduced. Nephilim."

Braedon shook his bag of popcorn. "Yeah, I've heard this theory from a few preachers. But average size people were buried in the mounds, too. Right?"

Cassie nodded. "In some mounds, the average-sized people were arranged around the body of the giant as if they were killed and buried to accompany him in death. Also, I learned a few of their giants were buried in metal breastplates and surrounded by jewelry and tools tempered by fire."

"Then, why didn't our textbooks and schools teach these things?" Charity asked.

"Good question, Charlie," Braedon stated.

"Beats me. Maybe the educators considered these were merely rumors and nothing more." Cassie popped the marshmallow into her mouth.

Zak cleared his throat. "Take your time to chew, sis, and don't get choked."

Taking a couple of seconds to eat and swallow, Cassie grimaced. "Thank you, *Mother*."

He sent her a wry grin. "You're welcome."

During their conversation, Olivia left the youngsters and settled herself on the ground next to Zak's chair, taking the opportunity of a pause in their discussion to voice her opinion. "Well, I think it's a travesty that the bodies were removed from the mounds. Think about it. They could have examined the bodies without removing them. Right where they lay."

"Seriously? In the mounds, Livie?" Braedon chided.

"Yeah. Good grief, Bray! It was a burial site!" she cried out. "Could I have a marshmallow to roast?"

Zak handed her the rod he had just prepared for himself. "Sure thing, Sweet Cheeks."

Olivia blushed as she accepted his gracious offer and snuck a glance up to his fire-lit face.

Quiet prevailed for a moment as Braedon and Charity exchanged stunned expressions.

Having swallowed the last of her next treat, Cassie studied each of their faces. Coughing, she continued with her earlier train of thought. "The most astonishing bit of info, though, is the fact there are ancient earthworks in shapes of triangles, octagons, etcetera, indicating construction by an advanced race."

"This would have been long before Pythagoras!" her brother noted.

"Precisely." Cassie stuck another marshmallow on the tip of her rod.

"Wow!" the other three exclaimed excitedly.

Charity's serious tone of voice expressed her interest. "I know we are focusing on this article and its theme right now, but let's check on some of these earthworks for possible future projects."

"Future projects?!" Zak stared at her.

"Sure," Charity replied. "You never know what the future holds."

"Especially with you, Charity! You, my friend, are unpredictable." Zak tossed popcorn up and caught it with his open mouth.

Cassie smiled. "Oh, come on, Zak. You're never bored around Charity." Turning to her best friend, she stated emphatically, "You never know what the future holds unless the Lord is leading you."

Eyes gleaming in the firelight, Braedon grinned in Charity's direction.

She broke the silence by clearing her throat. "Anyone for s'mores?" She pulled graham crackers and chocolate bars from a canvas bag leaning against her chair. Punkin, on the other side, raised his head and perked up his ears. "Not for you, Punkin. Chocolate is poison to dogs."

Punkin lowered his head again, his brown eyes still looking up at her.

"Ha *ha*!" Zak projected his voice dramatically toward her. "You let us fill up on popcorn and marshmallows first, saving all the chocolate for yourself, Charity. We're too full now!"

Cassie rebuked him, "We're *never* too full for chocolate, Zak!"

Everyone laughed at Zak's slumped posture and pretended pout. Still laughing, they started calling the children to come and enjoy the s'mores.

Having walked Adrianna to her aunt's house where she would spend the day with Willow, Charity now sat on the porch at home, dressed in a green checkered blouse pulled over faded blue jeans. She waited for Braedon to show up to go hiking with her. It was a perfect morning to climb through the woods, clear and crisp. She breathed in the sweet fragrance of magnolia and sweet pea vines wafting in the breeze. She had packed two thermoses with coffee along with chicken salad sandwiches loaded with tomatoes and lettuce and wrapped in special foil into her backpack in anticipation of a long, and, hopefully, adventurous day. She hadn't felt this giddy since she was a kid. Her excitement surprised and alarmed her. Was it because she hadn't hiked in a long time or because she was going hiking with Braedon? She was certain she should curb any such emotion since she would head back to work at the end of summer.

Gazing up into the azure sky and white wispy clouds, she thanked God for His creations. A blue jay called out to his mate, and a cardinal flew down to perch on the side banister. She remembered the scripture quoting Jesus saying, "My Father sees every sparrow that falls." How long had it been since she entertained such thoughts about her Heavenly Father? Too long, no doubt. Was it due to the fact she was home, surrounded by nature, recalling her early love and appreciation of Almighty God and His son, Jesus, who proved His love for the Father and mankind by going all the way to the cross?

The thump of Punkin's tail on the porch boards and the rumble of Braedon's truck interrupted her thoughts. As he pulled into the drive, his broad smile set her heart skipping crazily. *Get a grip, Charity!* she chastised herself. *You are not a teenager any longer, and you and Bray settled this thing called romance a long time ago. Don't make a fool out of yourself now!*

His gray t-shirt clung to his muscular chest as he swung out of the truck and wrapped his arms around Punkin as the dog threw his body into them. Like her, he was wearing his hiking boots and faded jeans.

She calmed her silly heart enough to greet him. "Hey, what's in *your* backpack?"

"Coffee and roast beef sandwiches," he responded.

"Well, we're going to be swimming in coffee, then. I packed two thermoses of coffee and chicken salad sandwiches!"

Braedon chuckled. "We may need every bite and all the coffee we can drink before this day is over."

She smiled in anticipation.

Watching Punkin running ahead of them, they strode toward the section of land where the creek flowed freely and swiftly over the smooth stones. Braedon held her hand as he helped her find jutting rocks on which to step across the stream to the bank sprinkled with the heavy scent of honeysuckle vines. They gave each other grins at the sight of Punkin splashing and lapping at the water before waiting patiently for them on the other side, his tail wagging, encouraging them to hurry. Even he settled down, sniffing the ground when they slowly began their ascent into the woods to the top of the mountain.

They stopped to catch their breath and enjoy the wooded environment. As the sunlight glimmered through the green leaves and peeked around their stems when a breeze separated their foliage, Charity became aware of Braedon staring at her face. "Why do you keep staring at me, Bray? Something on your mind?"

"Yeah. You're not wearing make-up today. Your face is fresh-scrubbed."

"So?"

"So, I can see the sprinkling of freckles across your shiny nose like when we were kids."

"They're not *that* noticeable."

"Just enough that they bring back memories, that's all." He turned his head away. But then, with two fingers, he lifted her chin and examined her face. "And it's good to see those thick blond eyelashes again instead of the spider legs coated with mascara."

She fought it, but his words rankled. She swept away his hand with one of her own. "Are you making fun of me?"

"No! I..."

"What about the hairline scar on your chin?" she interrupted. "Are you trying to hide it under that five o'clock shadow"

"That's a badge of courage I wear proudly through life."

"Oh, yeah? As I recall, you were running from me when a tree root protruding from the ground tripped you, and you fell flat on your face. The sharp point of a rock cut your chin." She lifted his chin with the palm of her hand and held it there. "You had to have stitches, and the cut left a scar." She moved closer to see it better. "It's faded and hidden by your scant beard, but I know it's there." She slowly traced the almost invisible line with the index finger of her other hand.

His lips gave her a crooked grin, and their eyes locked, at first in amusement, but the longer they gazed into each other's eyes, affection deepened the intensity and kept them close. He covered the hand touching his face with the warmth of his own. She finally shook off the trance-like gaze and turned away, appearing to scrutinize the branches of a tree. His hand reached out for her, his fingers clasping hers as he drew her attention elsewhere.

Charity felt reluctant to let go of the warmth of Braedon's hand when he withdrew to point out the animal tracks Punkin sniffed. Every once in a while, one or the other would stop to pick up rocks or dig out fossils with their pocket knives, standing head to head examining them. Rabbits played hide and seek through the brush.

Woodpeckers paused in their staccato pecking to watch the strangers invading their territory. As the couple stepped as quietly as their boots would allow, she couldn't resist the nagging curiosity whenever she saw an occasional hole they had to step around or hop over. It was a good thing they were climbing carefully, looking for Nature's wondrous gifts. She ignored the holes in favor of enjoying their trek up the mountain together.

As the two finally reached the top, where they found Punkin standing majestically on a massive boulder that jutted out over a cliff, they decided to eat lunch there. "Okay," Charity ventured. "Which coffee are we going to drink, and what sandwiches should we eat? And did you think to bring water? I didn't."

"All right, to answer your last question first, " Braedon began, "I did think to bring bottled water."

"Whew!" Charity blew her damp bangs back from her face. "I'm glad one of us had their mind on the reality of the hike! I'm hot and thirsty now!"

"I'll agree. You're pretty hot anytime!" Braedon teased in a husky voice and wiggled his eyebrows. Laughing at the wry expression in her narrowed eyes and tightened lips, he admitted, "I'm thirsty, too." He poured water into a tin cup for Punkin to lap up.

Taking long swigs from their water bottles, they pulled sandwiches out of their backpacks. "What are you in the mood for, Charlie, chicken salad or roast beef?" Braedon held up the beef sandwich as if tempting her.

"Chicken salad. That's why I packed it." She smiled. "What are you in the mood for?"

"That's a loaded question." He stopped teasing when her eyes rolled upward."Sorry, I guess that's enough of *that* for you. I want my roast beef with mustard. How 'bout coffee?"

"Why don't we each drink our own for now?" she suggested.

"Good idea," he agreed before handing a roast beef sandwich to Punkin, sitting patiently on his haunches, wagging his tail.

Busy eating, they spoke little as they sat on the edge of the boulder, enjoying the view of the wildflowers in the meadow and the creek flowing below them.

"Well, are you ready to explore the far and backside of your property?"Braedon broke the silence while repacking his large and well-stuffed bag.

She began to straighten her own bag. Slipping the straps onto her shoulders, she made sure it nestled securely in the center of her slender back. "As ready as I'll ever be."

He held out his hand to help her step down from the boulder.

She automatically placed her hand in his, feeling the warmth of his touch. When she stepped off the boulder, she lost her balance and would have fallen if he hadn't tightened his grip and draped his other arm around her waist, drawing her close in one swift motion. She gasped when she lost her equilibrium. Once she regained her composure, she looked up at him and caught an intense expression darkening his eyes. A frightful thrill coursed through her body, and her heart fluttered as if taking wing, leaving her poor, besotted mind behind. It was surely only a minute or two, but it seemed like time froze while she tried to tether her emotions.

Finally, he stood her on solid, level ground and held her at arm's length, placing his hands on her shoulders and looking past her into the sky. His voice sounded hoarse as he stated, "We'd better get going while we have bright sunlight to guide us through the woods."

All she could manage was a nod and a weak, "Okay."She could have kicked herself all the way around and down to the foot of the boulder. *What a fool I am,* she scolded herself. *I've become an emotional idiot.*

Losing my husband and then my mother, I let my heart run wild or fly in the face of consequences.

Punkin's barking cut into her self-recrimination. His fur was all but standing on end, and his muscles quivered as he took off chasing a rabbit around a tree. He almost banged his head when the rabbit escaped into a crevice under the boulder. He sniffed loudly, digging for all he was worth without success in dislodging the stone that had set there for decades, if not centuries.

Charity's tone of voice sounded forceful from bawling herself out mentally. "Punkin! Come here. Now!"

The dog turned at the command, hearing the authority behind it. He trotted sheepishly over to her and looked up expectantly.

"Let's go," she called in a more tender tone.

The dog wagged his tail as the three of them set off again through the trees.

Feeling awkward at the silent way they moved around the trees, she sneaked glances in Braedon's direction. She noticed he remained quiet even when she stopped with her pocket knife in hand to dig up and examine a small rock that looked like an arrowhead. She thought it odd when he didn't comment about the authenticity of it. She kept the question of whether it was an arrowhead or merely a rock in the shape of one to herself.

"Hey, do you see that?!" Braedon's voice exploded in her ears, causing her to literally jump.

"Wha...what? I don't see anything except trees, bushes, and vines."

"Exactly! Look to your left. You see vines, right?"

"Yeah."

"Yeah! Growing straight up and climbing over!"

"A rock formation?" She guessed.

He grinned at her. "Something even better. A stone construction!" He strode forward. "Come here. Let's pull some vines away and see what kind it is." He threw his backpack down, unzipped a compartment, and took out gloves.

Following his example, she did the same. Soon, they were pulling vines down with all their might as Punkin sat back on his haunches, watching them work. It wasn't very long until the sight of an old stone construction loomed in front of them.

"Do you know what this is?" Braedon asked, not taking his eyes off the wonder.

"No, I honestly don't."

"It's a wine cellar! A very old wine cellar."

Now, she looked with interest at the three oval doorways. Curious, she walked up to them, sliding her hands over the stones. As she approached the wooden doorways, worn with age, as if to enter, Braedon pulled her back.

"It's not safe in there, Charlie," he warned. "Something could collapse. Snakes could attack you in there since dense vines covered it for years. Any number of things could happen to you in there!"

She hesitated, but the desire to explore was strong. She pulled away, but he yanked her back, his protective nature stronger than her desire to examine the unknown. They each picked up their backpack, she with an angry flourish. She was obviously peeved at him as they walked on.

CHAPTER 12

S *he thinks I'm a wimp,* he thought in dismay. *Still, I couldn't let her risk her health by going into a place deserted for years and given over to rodents and snakes. Could I?*

Charity shook her head when he mentioned resting and taking time to eat. "Let's get to the house, wash up and eat at the table to finish off our sandwiches and coffee."

He readily agreed, hoping her mood would change by then.

As they neared the house, he began to wonder if he should stay or not. Watching her unlock the front door and press the buttons on the alarm, he decided he should stay and try to regain their camaraderie. He allowed Punkin to squeeze around him and go straight to his water bowl in the corner of the breakfast nook, loudly lapping until he flopped down onto his side to sleep. Braedon started to sit in a chair at the little round table, but Charity stopped him with a weary tone of voice.

"Let's eat in the dining room."

He felt his eyebrows raise and couldn't mask the surprise he felt. "Isn't that kinda formal, Charlie?"

"Wait 'til you see the table. It's still piled with papers and books around my laptop."

"Is there room for our sandwiches and thermoses?"

"We'll make room. I need the stimulus of all that paraphernalia right now. Besides, I'm going to make fresh coffee. It will taste much better in mugs." She turned to look at him for a few seconds."Don't you want to go wash up in the downstairs bathroom, and come into the kitchen for cold water first?"

"Now that you mention it, that's exactly what I'd like to do."

He could hear her running water as she washed her hands and prepared to make coffee. *How do I get US back? Our easy-going friendship back? This is frustrating the socks off me! Friendly one minute, intense the next, and then...cold. Yes...COLD! Help me, Lord. I'm falling in love with Charity, and I don't know how to encourage her to make the transition with me. I don't want to lose our friendship. I don't want to lose HER.*

Finally seated at the dining room table, they looked across the table at each other.,

"I'm sorry," they both began apologizing, not hearing what the other had to say.

Red-faced, Braedon grinned and gestured with open palms. "Ladies first."

"Okay." She blushed. "I'm sorry I acted like a spoiled brat."

"Not a spoiled brat," he grinned. "A headstrong journalist full of curiosity." He folded his arms and inspected the ceiling. "You must think I'm a wimp."

It was her turn to grin and shake her head. "Not a wimp. An overly protective father-brother-friend."

He winced at her description. He bowed his head as if in defeat and lowered his voice. "Is that what you think of me? Is that what I am to you? Just a father-brother-friend figure?"

Charity's blue eyes widened as a lock of dark hair fell onto his forehead. She felt a desire to place her hands on either side of his face and lift it to her own to softly kiss those pouting lips. She wanted to say, *No, I think you are the most attractive man I've ever met and who I need in my life longer than I planned.*

When he raised his eyes, they suddenly changed from a solemn darkness to glistening pools of light.

Was she imagining tears welling up in his eyes? Or was it a reflection of the ornate blue and white lamp above their heads? Could he actually read her thoughts? All she could answer was a soft whisper. "No, you're not just a father-brother-friend figure to me. You are my best friend."

"Yeah?" He questioned as if her expression belied her words. "What about Cassie? I thought she was your best friend."

"Sh...she...*is*. But *you* are my bestie, okay?"

He shook his head. "We sound like kids again, Charlie."

A serious and open expression transfigured her face. She gazed into his eyes. "But we are not kids, Bray. If we keep going like this, it could destroy our perfect friendship and our careers."

"How so?"

She saw he wasn't going to let it go. He must know he had her nibbling at the line as in fishing, and now that he had seen the look registered all over her face, he wasn't going to let her swim upstream without him. "I don't actually know. But let's take this... whatever it is...slow. Okay?"

"If we must." He stood and gazed down at her. "Think I'd better go?"

She smiled warmly. "Guess so." She walked through the living room into the sunroom with him and stood in front of the door with her hand on the knob. The toe of one of her boots brushed something on the floor. Bending down, her fingers felt the one end of a postcard sticking out from under the door. Braedon edged up beside her for a closer look. Letters cut from newspapers and magazines stated: **I know what you're here for. Go home.**

Charity frowned as she looked up at Braedon, who rolled his eyes. She caught his thoughts as if thrown in the air. They both groaned in exasperation and, together, identified the sender in one dry voice. "*Luna.*"

"Just forget it, Charlie." Braedon lowered his head for a soft kiss on her cheek. "Take a long bath and read a good book."

She nodded. "Think I'll do just that." She opened the door and stood on tiptoe to return the soft kiss to his cheek.

The next morning, as light filtered through the bedroom curtains, Charity groggily pulled back the covers and slipped her feet into the heelless, flat slippers. She grabbed her old blue robe at the foot of the bed, letting it hang loose over her checkered pajamas. Descending the carpeted stairs, she paused on the first landing where her mother's body had been found, very much aware of the quiet in the house. She remembered the girls had begged to stay overnight together at her aunt's house.

She found Punkin still lying next to his bowls in the breakfast nook. Sadness washed over her when she realized he had aged through the years and had exerted himself for her benefit - to keep her company – to be what she expected of him. Her thoughts seemed to awaken him.

He raised his beautiful brown head, a white streak glistening down the bridge of his nose. His soft brown eyes looked at her in anticipation and love. She knelt, lacing her fingers through the fur on either side of his head, and lowered her head to his. He wagged his white-tipped tail and licked her cheek. She then stood and held the back door open for him to go do his business.

After pouring her coffee into a large white mug, Charity joined Punkin out on the front porch. Settled in the rocker, ready to relax and enjoy the morning air and birdsongs, she heard instead a silver car turning into her drive. Bracing in embarrassment at being seen in her disheveled state with bed hair, she rose to her feet, her hands wrapped around her coffee mug for comfort and courage.

A man with thinning white hair, wearing a gray pinstriped suit and white shirt with a black and white patterned tie, approached her steps. Another younger man with darker, fuller hair, looking business-like in a navy suit, light blue shirt, and bluish-cream colored-swirl tie, followed him.

"May I help you?" she asked in as much of a cool tone as her unkempt appearance would permit.

"Ms. Payne?"

"Yes?"

"Forgive me for disrupting your morning. I'm Mr. Stevens, and this is one of our attorneys, Mr. Martino." He cleared his throat. "I've tried to call you many times and sent letters to your mother. I'm sorry for your loss, but I hope we can complete our business and get out of your way."

Aware of the fact that she knew he did not call, she raised her eyebrows. "Business?"

"Yes. Your mother and I agreed on the sale of this place to my corporation. Unfortunately, and sadly, she passed before the transaction could be completed. You just need to sign the papers, and we'll get out of your w-."

A booming voice interjected before she could reply or ask a question. "You'll get out of her way, any way, Stevens!"

Roy strode from around the house and stood, hands on his hips. He suddenly wiped a hand down his navy blue shirt as if it were soiled from the conversation while his other pointed binoculars in their direction. "You're not going to trick this young lady into signing anything so you can build that shopping center. Her mother did no such thing. She told you no." He glared daggers at the two men. "Now, you get off this property!"

"I think the little lady can answer for herself!" Mr. Stevens countered vehemently. "Besides, Mr. Martino, here, was present when I talked with her mother and witnessed the agreement. Isn't that right?" he asked pointedly to his partner.

Charity watched as Mr. Martino lowered his eyelids.

She took a deep breath. "Mom never said anything to me about agreeing to sell, Mr. Stevens. And we talked on the phone nearly every day."

"Did she ever mention my letters, calls, or visits?"

"No, not at all."

"Well, then, there you go. She probably didn't think it was any of your business since you lived elsewhere."

"That doesn't sound like my mother, sir."

Mr. Stevens squared his shoulders. "Well, you can't stop progress, Ms. Payne!"

Again, Roy beat her to a reply. "Oh, yes, she can, Mr. Stevens. She can stop anything on her own property. No use making your spiel about the glories of the shopping center and how many people it will put to work. Don't try to tell her she is selfish to refuse, the way you accused her mother."

Charity's cheeks flamed red on hearing that. "Think it's time for you to go, Mr. Stevens. Have a good trip back."

"Look, lady, we flew all the way here to offer you a stupendous price for this little stretch of land."

"Then you can fly right back. We're done here. Now go!"

At the angry tone of Charity's voice, Punkin stiffened on the top step and growled, showing teeth.

The two men made a hasty retreat to their rental car, drove in a circle spewing up dust, and sped away toward the intersection.

She turned an exasperated look to Roy. "Thank you for intervening. I knew nothing about this."

"Nothin' to know. They sent letters your mom tore up, called, and finally came in person. She said no to their offer."

"It's a good thing you happened by. You clarified a lot of things for me." She inhaled a deep breath and let it out in a sigh. "I hate to admit it, but I would have been too stunned to know exactly what to do."

He averted his face and coughed. "I was walkin' through the woods, watchin' birds through my binoculars, when I saw them get out of the car. I figured they were up to no good."

He started to leave but turned around. "I don't mind you sellin' the property, Charity, if that's what you intend to do. Jus' don't mess up our peaceful countryside with another shoppin' center. We already have a nice one in Charleston, Southridge, and others in the opposite direction."

"I wouldn't think of doing that, Roy. I promise you," she answered him quickly. "Would you like a cup of coffee?"

"Nah, thank you, though. My nephew's waitin' for me to show him a few repairs I need done on my old house."

A young man with dark blond hair and sporting purposely faded denim marked by strategically placed holes met him a few yards away. Roy yelled, "This here's my nephew, Henry." He slapped the teenager on the back. Henry rolled his eyes as if the introduction wasn't necessary, or he was bored with it as Charity waved from the porch. Punkin growled.

"Okay, Punkin, I've received enough company in my lovely PJs. I'm going to get dressed, and we're heading into town."

Punkin wagged his white-tipped tail as if to say that was a good idea and followed her into the house.

CHAPTER 13

A robins-blue sky greeted Charity as she drove on the main road into town. She enjoyed viewing wildflowers, trees, creeks, and distant hills. Nostalgia enveloped her at the sight of horses and cows grazing in pastures enclosed by white fences. She stopped for gas at the local garage before passing the family-owned restaurant on the same road. She finally turned onto Brick Street, where a two-story department store set on the left corner and the bank on the right. Beyond that building, the police and fire departments spread out on the main road. Before stopping anywhere, she wanted to see the large hardware-general store and the beauty salon on the left, the wonderfully familiar ice cream shop and connecting drugstore on the right. Happy memories filled her mind of her mother always taking her in for a treat of their favorite hot fudge sundae when they went into town to shop and, later, as a teen, meeting there with her friends in the evening before catching a movie at the theater on the far corner of Galligher Avenue.

She also saw the newly built county branch library on the right corner where Galligher Avenue intersected. Across the avenue, on the left corner and adjacent to the library, stood the tall City Hall. On the right corner, across from the library, the Post Office doors displayed posters. On up, past the avenue, she could see the building on the left still housed the doctor, dentist, and law offices, as indicated by the signs out front. She was pleased to see that a jewelry store and flower shop had been added on the right, where there had been a vacant lot used for traveling carnivals and town fairs. She supposed Country Lanes now held their festivals on another street or the outskirts of town. As she backed up and turned her vehicle around at the end of the street, she noticed the well-spaced houses on both sides of the road. She already knew by heart the layout of the streets and avenues named after the first residential families and mayors. Pulling into a parking space in front of the ice-cream shop, she opted for one of their sandwiches instead of the locally famous hotdogs and picked up one for Punkin. She sipped her cola as she jotted down a list of supplies she needed from the hardware store.

Leaving Punkin in the car, with windows partially lowered, she entered the vast building which carried everything from tools, farming equipment, and work clothes to plants. There were straight, wide concrete aisles on which one could always see the large empty space at the back and its double doors leading to the paved alley.

"Charity Payne! You seem to follow me everywhere I go!" Roy Galligher laughed. "What brings a city gal into a farmer's paradise?"

She grinned in his direction. "I have a whole list of supplies to pick up." She waved the sheet of paper.

"Like what?"

"Well, a shovel for one thing. And a hoe and...." She looked down at the list. "Oh, yeah... a rake."

"Oh..." He gave her an odd look as he narrowed his eyes. "Why is that?"

"Dad's shovel, hoe, and rake rusted, rotted, and fell apart."

"No, I mean, why do you need them? What do you plan to do with them?"

"Don't know, but I want to have a shovel, hoe, and rake in any case."

"What happened? Did your mother leave her's out to rust in the weather?"

"Well, apparently she did." Roy was acting awfully strange over such commonplace tools everyone in the area used. "I found them leaning against the side of the garage." Tired of all the questions, she shifted her body to end the conversation. "I'm going to check out the flowers while I'm here, too."

He grinned. "Yep, they still have some good plants left. Well, I guess I'll see you around."

She nodded and moved down an aisle. She made a mental note to stop at the grocery store on the main road and hoped she didn't run into him there again. Sad. They'd all been such good friends in the past, and now their conversation felt awkward. Why?

Once at home, while Punkin ran around sniffing and exploring, obviously glad he could run free, Charity planted marigolds in front of her porch banisters. She spent the remainder of the day sorting out the notes on the Adena mounds and matching up pictures on her dining room table.

When will my daughter want to come home? Adrianna had begged to stay at Bray's with Willow. If Charity didn't have flowers to plant and her project to work on, the quiet in the house would be unbearable.

Cassie called the next morning before Charity could brew coffee. She sounded a little troubled and asked if her best friend would meet her for lunch at the restaurant in town.

"Are you sure you wouldn't rather have lunch here, Cas?"

"No, I think we need a break, Charity. A girl's afternoon out, so to speak. Do you mind?"

"Oh, no, not at all. How about noon?"

"Thank you, Charlie. Old times and all that...."

Checking the time, Charity quickly brewed coffee and took her cup and wheat toast out on the back porch to avoid being seen by any more unexpected company too rude to call. Rising to go inside to shower, she propped the screen door open for Punkin, but he raised his head and looked steadily at her, then curled up tighter to sleep. Taking her time, letting the warm water splash onto her face and over her body, she then towel dried and wrapped a terry cloth around her hair. She sat at the dresser, drying her hair with the blow-dryer, and thinking about the troubled tone in Cassie's voice.

Before setting the alarm, she opened the back door to see if Punkin wanted to come inside. He only looked at her and chose the soft breeze and peace of the back porch. She placed his bowl of water in a shady corner, knelt to ruffle his fur, and told him she would be back soon. He put a paw on her hand and gave her a brown-eyed look of love.

Cassie was already sitting at a table, nervously fingering the blue-checkered table cloth, when Charity entered the restaurant. Even the yellow sundress couldn't brighten the sad expression on her face. Charity's lime-green dress caught her attention, and she forced a smile.

"Hey."

"Hey, yourself, girl. Why the glum expression? What's going on?"

"Nothing. That's the problem."

Charity pulled out a chair and sat down. "Problem?"

"I have no life. Well, no life of my own. The only thing interesting is your project. I'm living *your* life."

"You're a teacher. A good one, too- I've heard you teaching your Sunday School class. Aren't you happy teaching anymore?"

"Yeah. I like teaching, but I'm not...well...I'm not fulfilled. I'm tired of reading other authors' words and showing other artists' picture books to children."

"What would you like to do?"

"I'd like to create my own children's books that make youngsters smile and teach them a thing or two through them."

"Then why don't you do that?"

"Mother."

Charity arched an eyebrow. "What does your mother have to do with your decision?"

"She's proud I'm a teacher like her. Yes, she taught high school, and now, she's retired. But...but...Charlie...she is living vicariously through *me*, now."

A young waitress with a cute brown haircut stood impatiently, poised with a small clipboard and pen. "Are you two ready to order now?"

Both young women looked down at their menus, somewhat embarrassed. Charity spoke first, "I'm sorry. Yes, I'll take the grilled chicken and rice dinner with iced tea."

Cassie nodded. "I'll take the same except with mac and cheese and cola, please."

"Okay. Be back in a few minutes with your food," the now-satisfied waitress assured them cheerfully.

"Okay, take this advice with a grain of salt since had I stayed and worked in this area, I would have lived with Mom." Charity held up a hand between the friends. "But I think it might be time you moved out of your mother's house into a place of your own and let your mother rediscover her own interests. Pursue the life which fulfills you. Maybe it's your calling, Cas. After all, you are super-talented. God gave you gifts to use. So use them!"

Visibly encouraged, Cassie brightened. "I'll have to pray about the move and quote *calling*, but I will definitely consider this. She wants to keep a tight reign on me for some reason."

"Could it be because she lost your older sister after her horse threw her when it saw that snake?"

"Bailey has been gone for several years now."

"Yes, but losing her oldest daughter suddenly...think about it... She watched as Bailey suffered while that horrible bruise on her leg turned to gangrene. You know she's not over Bailey's death."

Tears filled Cassie's eyes. "But she seemed strong afterward, Charlie. She even stood in church telling how Bailey saw angels in the room and knew her spirit was leaving with them."

"I'm sure she told others the account of Bailey's passing because she felt her sweet daughter would want her to be strong and share her experience. It was a comfort for her to tell it. And reminding herself aloud reinforced her resolve to stay strong. Yet, in her private moments of painful loss, she also had to grieve. That is only human."

Cassie nodded. "You're right...."

"Yet, I still think you should move out –maybe someplace nearby- to give yourself an opportunity to pursue your dreams and allow your mother to discover her own identity again. It's merely my opinion. But you are the one who should decide what is best for you."

"You don't know how grateful I am for your input, Charlie." Cassie fixed her eyes earnestly on Charity's. "I'll need to ask God's guidance."

"Why don't we pray now?" Charity reached out her hands.

"Now? Here?"

"Yep, right here. And we can thank the Lord for our food and our time together."

When they raised their heads, they saw the waitress holding a tray of warm dishes and smiling down at them. It was then they noticed the tiny, glistening cross on a thin gold chain around her neck and her nametag. They smiled back at her as she placed the plates before them and promised to bring their drinks.

"Thank you, Trish," Charity said sincerely.

"You're most welcome." The waitress' smile broadened as she moved away, appreciating the acknowledgment.

Feeling rejuvenated, as always when she and Cassie enjoyed girl-time together, she headed straight for the back porch when she returned home. Punkin wasn't sitting or lying anywhere there, nor was he in the yard. "Punkin, Boy, where are you?" She called his name all around the house and grounds. She stopped in her tracks as she scanned the large field and the edge of the woods. "Where did you go, Boy?!"

She whipped her phone from the side pocket of her purse. She could hardly wait for someone to answer.

"Hi ya, Sunshine!" Braedon's voice sang in her ear.

"Hi, yourself, Bray. Is Punkin there with the girls and you?"

"Nope. But let me check outside. Did you check the barn and garage?"

"Doing that now, but still don't see or hear him."

She could hear the squeak of Braedon's screen door opening and the rustling as he stepped out onto his porch and down the steps. "I'm walking the perimeter of the property," he breathed into the phone. "But don't see him anywhere around here. Of course, he could still be in the woods, though, if he took a shortcut."

She, too, walked through fields, her eyes searching the banks across the creek along the edge of the woods.

"Hey, girl, give him some time to show someplace. Maybe he decided to visit your aunt or..." he stopped talking.

"Or what?"

"Or, maybe, he went a-courtin'. Ever thought of that?"

"He's too old for that, Bray."

"Says who? You?"

"In dog-days, he is much too old to go *a-courtin'*."

"Okay, perhaps he went *visitin'* his girlfriend then."

"Oh, Bray, is that *all* you think about?!"

"No. But courtin' is a part of life, Charlie, and a good possibility. It's not like he's been gone days or weeks." He grew quiet for a few seconds and then asked, "Are you lonely, Charlie?"

"Lonely? Me? Why would I be lonely? I have this big house to clean and clear besides finishing our project. I'm not lonely. Just missing Punkin, worried and aggravated that I can't find him. He's getting older, Bray, and our romp through the woods wore him out for hours."

Bray's voice softened. "I'll keep an eye out for him, Charlie, and the girls can help search the roads on our way to your house this evening."

Her own voice softened. "Thank you, Bray. I'll call if he shows up here."

"Same here. Now, you just relax. He'll probably come home soon, scratching on the door and looking sheepish." When she didn't reply, he simply said, "See you later."

"Later, Bray."

On her walk back to the house, Charity phoned her aunt only to learn Florie hadn't seen Punkin either. Exhaling a big sigh, she went inside to make coffee. With her plans short-circuited, she would sit on the back porch, inhaling the scent of magnolia blossoms and sip vanilla-creamed coffee and...wait...

About dusk, she heard Braedon's truck pull up out front and the chatter of the two young girls. She rounded the house and was saddened to see the disappointment etched on her friend's face as he shook his head.

Braedon held up a bag. "We searched the roads when we picked up burgers and fries. If Punkin doesn't come tonight, your aunt says she'll be glad to keep the kids while we take Livie and go to nearby farms to ask if folks have seen him." He paused. "If they haven't, we could search the woods in case he chased an animal who burrowed itself in a crevice, and he is standing guard waiting for it to come out. Is that okay with you, Charlie?"

"Of course." She began feeling more hopeful and determined to give the girls a good evening. "Let's eat at the round table in the back-yard. Maybe the smell of food will draw him home." She deliberately exerted the effort to chuckle.

"Sure," Braedon agreed. "He might have chased a rabbit too far, and it's just taking him time to get home."

"Or a squirrel," the girls chimed together, delighted they had the same thought at the same time. They giggled.

"Or a squirrel," Braedon repeated. "Though squirrels usually climb a nearby tree. A cat does, too, but sometimes they take off at a run. A cat can run a long way before he tries to find a safe shelter."

"Yeah," Charity whispered. "He could have chased a cat." She was ready to hang onto hope. Then why did this empty feeling persist? "It *is* still early," she stated to convince herself.

"Have you checked to see what the cameras may have caught?" He looked surprised when she grimaced and shook her head.

"I'm afraid I'm still not used to having this kind of technology." She blushed with another confession. "I'm afraid I often forget to set the alarm, too." Her shoulders drooped.

Probably, in order to lift her spirits and change her self-recriminating attitude – to dissipate her feeling of stupidity – he said, "That's understandable, Charity. You never thought you would need such precautions, especially here." But he immediately suggested, "Let's take a look-see now, though."

She knew him well enough to know his words were honest, but mostly meant to make her feel better about herself. And she did, indeed, feel better. She straightened up in her seat and agreed whole-heartedly. "Let's do it!"

Setting the video on the desired date, they observed the hours she was gone that day. They could have fast-forwarded the footage, and both were obviously tempted, but their eyes were glued to the back porch where Punkin lay curled in the corner and the back yard. It seemed like hours to them even though it wasn't, and Charity's mind began to wander. Then, Punkin's position on the porch changed. He lay with his front legs pointed toward the back steps. She froze the video. Her heart melted at the view of the brown fur on the top of his head between his perked-up ears. She could just barely make out the white streak down his snout to his black nose. *Was he looking for me to come home...waiting? And yet, I never came...not before he left. Did he go looking for me?"* Her heart broke at the thought. *Oh, Punkin, I wish I could have come home, hugged you around the neck, and told you how much I love you! Now, I don't know where you are, and your absence is a hole in my heart.*

When she started the video again, they saw Punkin rise, first with a wagging tail, then his whole body stiffened as he moved closer to the steps. She observed what must be a defensive stance and could imagine the growl that emitted from his throat as he bared his teeth. Narrowing their eyes and putting their heads together closer to the screen, they tried to see the black-clad figure that had stopped in the field. They froze the film again, examining the picture, but the figure was almost out of range to the left, and they couldn't identify him. Rerunning the video, they could see Punkin jumping off the steps and running toward the mysterious person until they were out of range.

Turning off the monitor, she scooted her chair back. "Could that person be Nick?"

Braedon backed up his chair, too, and seemed to be deep in thought. "If so..." He paused again in thought. "Maybe Punkin was just playing at being the big bad dog?"

"Didn't look like it, Bray."

Frowning, they looked into each other's eyes and faced the truth they would have liked to avoid.

"No, it didn't." He took a deep breath. "I'm sorry, Charlie."

CHAPTER 14

It felt strange going to bed without Punkin following Charity and Adrianna upstairs and lying beside one bed or another. Even the girls' giggling from the far end of the hall didn't dispel the gloom that hovered over her room. How many times did she peek out a window tonight or actually open the door to peer out onto the porches? She left bowls of water on both the front and back porch. She would have left dry dog food, but didn't relish the idea of creatures sneaking out of the woods for a snack.

Sometime before morning, she must have fallen asleep. She woke with a start, jumped out of bed and ran barefoot down the stairs, turned off the alarm, and flung open the front door. No Punkin on the front porch. She turned on her heel and ran through the house to the back door. She snapped on a light. The back porch was empty of life. No Punkin lay curled up there or under a tree. A weight fell to the pit of her stomach as she brewed coffee. "Don't give up, girl!" she commanded herself. "Bray will come, and we will ask neighbors, search the roads and even comb the woods, if necessary. Just hang in there, and stay calm." She decided to wear a pretty little dress and summer flats to cheer herself up. If her feet bothered her as they walked the country road, she would take off the shoes and go barefoot.

Everyone along the road shook their heads, saying they hadn't seen any dogs other than their own. That is until Braedon, Charity, and Olivia ran across their new friend, Nick. The tan shirtless boy in cut-off jeans looked at them curiously. The black and white family dog joined him in front of his grandmother's white three-story farmhouse, vigorously wagging her bushy tail. From what the boy had told Charity, she knew this mixed-breed dog stayed close to home and Nick's grandmother. If their dog suddenly disappeared, they would think something had happened to her.

"The last time I saw Punkin was yesterday afternoon. He was chasing some guy in a black hoodie toward the woods. Didn't he come back home?"

Charity and Braedon exchanged glances and looked toward the woods, shaking their heads.

"Where did they go into the woods, Nick?" Braedon asked with his eyes scanning the banks.

"Not here," the boy informed him.

Braedon turned to him. "You want to show us?"

"Sure. Do better than that. I'll go search with you."

The spot where Punkin entered the woods was closer to the house than first expected but, nevertheless, out of range of the cameras. Charity kept expecting him to burst through the bushes, rushing her into one of their big hugs. But it didn't happen. Hours of walking, climbing, and calling his name didn't work. No Punkin barged through the leaves, dancing around them. They didn't even hear a distant bark. Feeling physically drained, she could only hope they would find him at home, panting and wagging his tail, overjoyed to see his two favorite humans. But the yard and porches lay empty.

After Nick said goodbye and assured them he'd watch for the dog, he started off for home at a run. Livie took off to see if Punkin had made it to their house by now. Frustrated, Charity cried out to Braedon. "Where could he be, Bray?"

This time, Braedon only gazed at her in silence.

Staring at the neat front porch with its two rockers and the gray-painted floorboards empty of life, Charity leaned against the white post at the top of the steps in despair and pushed her feet into her shoes. Thinking Punkin could yet be making his way across the fields, she rounded the house. The fields waved in the breeze, but didn't offer a sight of her beloved canine moving through the tall grass. She scanned the empty back porch, her mind trying to conjure him up out of the wooden banisters and corners before turning to Braedon for comfort and reassurance.

He gently pulled her to his chest and stroked her hair. "It's okay, Charlie. Punkin may have followed a female dog home or gone to visit someone further away...someone he may have visited when he lived with your mother, perhaps one of her friends he came to know really well. It's still early...he hasn't been gone long enough for you to give up."

She raised her head, blue eyes searching his brown ones for a glimmer of hope. She closed her eyes as he lowered his face, his forehead touching hers. All she could feel was the need for his touch, the comfort of his closeness. The warmth of his breath as he spoke comforting words. Her arms circled his neck and his cheek pressed against her cheek. Feeling him draw back a little, she opened her eyes. The shadows playing around his whiskered jawline and mouth stirred her emotions. His dark eyes searched hers before he lowered his head again. Their lips touched hesitantly...tenderly and then melted into a sweet kiss.

They both drew back at the same time, and Braedon released his hold on her. Both stood red-faced.

"I'm sorry...," he began.

"No, I'm sorry, Bray. I gave in to my need for comfort and crossed the line."

"I'm the one who crossed the line, Charlie. Forgive me."

Now, she felt flustered, awkward. Was the only reason he kissed her because she forced herself upon him for reassurance? And he didn't know how to say no without hurting her? *Oh boy, what an ironic jab at my self-esteem!* "You didn't do anything wrong, Bray. We both know it was me." She sneaked him a wry smile.

"For our friendship's sake, you might want to rethink that, Charlie." His eyes locked with hers in a smoldering gaze. "Truth is, I've wanted to kiss you since the first day you came home."

Surprise overwhelmed her at his admission.

He grasped her gently by the shoulders. "I've probably ruined our friendship, but my desire to comfort you...our closeness...." He bowed his head and closed his eyes. "I took advantage of your situation."

She grabbed his arms before he could back off. "*We* took advantage of my situation, Bray." His eyes flew open as she continued, "My feelings for you deepened some time ago, but I dared not let you know."

"*Really?*" He grinned as she nodded in relief and satisfaction. His arms circled her waist again, and he embraced her. "I know you feel bad about Punkin's disappearance, but he wouldn't want us to be sad. Besides, he'll probably show up when we least expect it." Suddenly, he chuckled and shifted until his hands were on both sides of her waist and lifted her off her feet. "Maybe he's just playing match-maker." Looking up into her face, he announced, "This calls for a dinner date! Don't you think? *Before* the kids come home again?"

"Sounds like it!" She agreed, smiling down at him.

Excited as two teenagers on a first date, it didn't take either one of them long to separate and freshen up, changing into casual dress clothes. She wore a navy blue dress with little sprigs of pastel flowers decorating the design, and he, a button-down white shirt and black slacks. They were both relieved to realize Luna wasn't serving tables on this special night. They gazed across the table at each other as they had never allowed themselves to do in the past. Trish smiled at them as she took their order. They picked at their food, hardly aware of what they ate. They were still too astonished at the development in their friendship to do anything but stare into each other's eyes and talk softly about how they felt.

On the way back to the house, Charity made a quick phone call and managed to talk the girls into leaving Aunt Florie's to come home with them. Charity and Braedon both agreed that this was the wise thing to do since they were so caught up in their new relationship they dared not spend the rest of the evening alone.

"Let's check the house for you, Charlie, before Willow and I leave. Okay?"

"Is that necessary, Bray?" She expressed surprise.

"Well...," Braedon paused. "Maybe not necessary, but it's better to be safe than sorry, as they say. It's better to lean to the side of caution."

It did help to have people in the house, and Charity tossed the girls small bottles of soda before brewing a pot of coffee. She smiled as she heard Braedon's footsteps upstairs and the hinges of closet doors opening and closing.

Coming into the kitchen, he announced, "All clear."

"Thought so, but I wanted to humor you."

"Oh, you did, did you? Well, humor me some more," he teased, pulling her a little closer to give her a quick kiss.

"Oh my gosh!" The giggling shrieks of high-pitched voices caused the couple to jump apart, both smiling sheepishly.

Busying her embarrassed self by preparing their mugs, she suggested, "Let's take our coffee on the front porch while the girls watch one tv show before separating for the night."

"Why not a movie, Mom? Willow could stay tonight." Adrianna nearly whined.

"Uh...," Charity saw the pleading in her daughter's eyes and the hopeful expression on Willow's face. "Uh...you gals have to sleep sometime, and something tells me you two together probably talk long after your parent or Aunt Florie goes to sleep." She and Braedon carried their mugs past the girls. "Enjoy your tv program, girls."

Knowing their request got shot down, the daughters exchanged defeated glances before going into the family room.

The night sky displayed its array of stars. The full moon brightened the surrounding fields and sent a glow over the mountainous woods. They spoke softly while relaxing in the peace permeating the land.

Oh, Lord, Charity prayed, *I hope Punkin is at peace wherever he is.* Later tonight, before bed, she would look at the many pictures her Dad had taken of their German Shepherd Collie. Summer picnics, chasing balls or Frisbees. Holidays in front of the Christmas tree. She wanted to see, especially, the photo of her Dad sitting with Punkin on the top step of this porch. The dog always seemed to pose at such moments as if he knew what the camera was doing. If her Dad or she snapped one of him standing near the dogwood tree, he would wag his tail a few times and then hold perfectly still, looking into the camera until they lowered it.

As if reading her thoughts, Braedon reached with his free hand to clasp hers on the arm of the rocker.

"Just thinking of the pictures we took of Punkin from puppyhood on."

Braedon nodded. "I remember most of them." He gently squeezed her hand. "Your Dad enjoyed pointing a camera and catching him in all kinds of positions at every stage." He chuckled softly. "Even I took a few pics while he stayed with me. He tended to relish the attention as much as I enjoyed taking the photos."

She smiled tenderly and nodded her head. And sent another prayer up for their beloved fur-friend to have a peaceful night.

The next day, after checking the porches and peering out over the fields, she consoled herself with work on the project, keeping busy typing her article and sorting out the amazing photos Braedon had taken at sites. She focused on the information concerning the looters, theorizing what possible relics they may have carried off and what became of them. She didn't believe these men considered their loot stolen. After all, these were ancient burial sites of a culture long gone. The only reason they kept quiet and hid the items was that these mounds were set on particular pieces of property and, more than likely, that property did not belong to them. In some cases, it may have been the owners. The opening of the burial sites was initially crude until professional archeologists were called into the digs. Looters dug tunnels, and a few property owners charged the public a fee to enter.

Charity poured herself another mug of coffee. *Yep, and though there are items on display in the Smithsonian and smaller museums, there were relics and skeletons which never saw the light of day if one could believe the first descriptions of the findings in the early newspaper reports.* Propping her elbows on the table, she rubbed her temples. *No, they are either destroyed or hidden away. In storage?*

On Sunday morning, Charity dressed carefully for church, selecting a dress from her closet. It felt good to slip the soft blue material over her head and see the way it fell around her waist and hips in the mirror. She combed her hair into a loose chignon at the nape of her neck, leaving tendrils to dangle there and both sides of her face. Applying touches of foundation and powder, a bit of mascara, and lip gloss made her feel more feminine than her usual freshly washed face when she wore blue jeans and t-shirts. She slid her feet into heeled sandals, calling out to her daughter to hurry so they wouldn't be late.

Adrianna met her at the top of the stairs, wearing a white sleeveless blouse and pink skirt. "Mom, I really would've liked to have gone to Sunday School."

"I'm sorry, honey. I don't seem to be on schedule these days. A little too laid-back this summer," Charity answered as they descended the steps.

"You're working on another project, though." Adrianna reminded her.

"Yeah, you're right. I'm sorry, Sweetheart."

"Don't be, Mom. It gives Willow and me more time to hang out together. I just wish I'd gone to Sunday School with her. Cassie teaches our class. I think I would like it a lot."

"I'm sure you would. I'll try to do better next week. I promise."

At first, it felt weird to enter once again the church where her mother's body had lain in a coffin not too long ago. Practically the same people sat in the pews on that sad day. Cassie's wave caught her attention, and she and Adrianna took seats beside her and Zak. She felt a tap on her shoulder. Turning, she was pleased by Braedon wearing a gray suit and tie, smiling approvingly into her face. The girls giggled together as Charity motioned her own daughter to turn her attention toward the front when the choir director was about to lead the congregation through the opening hymn, *Showers of Blessings*. Her Aunt Florie hobbled out of the choir to balance herself with one hand and hold a microphone with the other. Her soprano voice filled the sanctuary with *Great is Thy Faithfulness*. Her singing voice never failed to surprise Charity as she sensed the Lord's presence the way she hadn't for years. The pastor looked distinguished in his navy blue suit and silver hair as his dignified posture commanded silent respect. His message referring to the Lord's Prayer pertained to forgiveness. Charity felt something calling her home where she belonged. She didn't know where this call was coming from. Childhood memories? Or regret that she hadn't visited her mother or this sweet little church often? The years had slipped by too fast, and now her parents were gone, and with them, the opportunity to join them for worship in their church. Even if she answered that call, would she ever feel the same here? Maybe, she could give her daughter the opportunity to worship here with her.

As people gathered around her in the aisle upon leaving, Roy took her by the arm and steered her aside. He spoke in a low, sympathetic voice. "Charity, I'm real sorry about Punkin."

She nodded her head, her heart suddenly heavy again. She knew he meant kindness, but it still hurt. "Have you seen him up at your place?"

He hesitated before answering her hopeful question. "Nah, I'm sorry, not up 'round my place."

"Please keep an eye out for him, Roy." Her gaze drifted past him. "I'm afraid he's trapped somewhere. I know he is getting old and probably won't live much longer, but...." A knot formed in her throat. "But with losing Mom so suddenly...this loss...this not-knowing aches my heart."

Roy coughed, and his eyes welled up in unshed tears. He appeared truly sorrowful about her misgivings.

Braedon interrupted. "Hey, Charlie, won't you and Adrianna join us for Sunday dinner? Your aunt and Julia will come if you do." His broad, white toothy smile dispelled the curtain of gloom that had draped itself over her heart. She needed his uplifting voice, the chatter of company, and the girls' laughter today.

However, the worry set in again on Monday, causing Charity to lay in bed staring at the ceiling. *Lord, it's the not-knowing that is bearing down on me. Wherever Punkin is, whatever has happened to him...I need to know. This not-knowing hurts more every day.*

She finally forced herself out of bed, but without showering, she listlessly slipped into faded jeans and a gray sweatshirt still hanging on the bed frame. She swept her hair up in a messy twist before sluggishly taking one step at a time down the carpeted staircase. She stood, gazing at first out the kitchen window over the sink, and then mug in hand, sat on the back porch, looking over the fields and along the edge of woods. Only a glimmer of hope for Punkin's return remained this morning. *Lord, I'm sorry. I can't pretend with you. I'm losing hope that Punkin is alive. But I need to know where he is and what has happened to him. Please, Lord, help me.*

"There you are, Charlie." Braedon's voice carried, pulling her from her silent prayer.

She shifted her eyes in his direction, but couldn't plaster a fake smile on her face. She managed a nod.

"I knocked at the front door and even rang the doorbell. The girls had me drop them at your Aunt Florie's. I hope you don't mind." He looked questioningly at her reticence as she shook her head. His dark eyes darted side to side and then lit up with an idea. "Hey, why don't we hike up to the rock again?" When she only took another sip of coffee, he added, "Or better yet, let's search the woods beyond the border of your property lines."

"Okay, Bray, but I'm not in the mood to eat today. Let's just take a couple of bottles of water, alright?"

"That'll be fine, Charlie. I ate a good breakfast already."

He sat down on the top step as she went inside to wash her face, brush her teeth, change into a floral printed tunic and comb her hair. She peered into the mirror as she applied a little lip gloss. Her reflection looked a bit better, but her sad expression gave her a gloomy appearance.

Tossing a couple of bottles of water into her first-aid backpack, she pushed the screen door open and let it slam shut behind her. "Ready?"

"Yeah, but don't you want to at least close your back door? And, maybe set the alarm?" he asked. "Here, I'll do it for you."

Her spirit still sinking, she felt like she was dragging her feet through mud as they began their trek through the woods. Passing through the shadow of the huge boulder overhead, they continued searching for signs of a dog until they were almost across Roy's property line. Dried leaves, twigs, and a few fallen branches were strewn at the base of most of the trees in that vicinity.

Suddenly, a tuft of brown fur caught Charity's attention. Her heart leaped at first before plummeting to the pit of her stomach as she neared the base of a tall elm tree. There, with his head resting against the tree as if he had fallen asleep, lay Punkin. Both she and Braedon stood silently transfixed.

She shook herself out of the shock of finally seeing the beloved object of their search laying lifeless at their feet and knelt as she'd always done, placing her fingers on top of his head and running them softly along the side of his face. Her hand automatically reached to rub his now stiff shoulder bone and along his white chest where she could see a prominent spot, dark with dried blood.

Braedon knelt beside her, examining the wound. "The wound is only a couple of days old. It's a good thing the temperatures turned cooler the last few days, and here, it must be at least five degrees cooler than down in the valley areas. We're blessed, too, that animals or birds didn't attack his body."

"Blessed, Braedon?" She lifted her head and arched an eyebrow.

"Yeah. As bad as this is, it could be worse." He stood upright, gazing down at his furry friend's body. "He didn't live long after the shot, Charlie. It looks like he passed peacefully."

She, too, stood up and whispered. "Who would want to hurt Punkin? Why? Everyone around here knew and liked him."

"I'm as mystified as you are."

"Whoever shot him didn't give me a chance to even say goodbye to him. I wasn't here for him, Bray!" A sob tore from her throat.

His voice deepened. "If you had been, you might be lying here with him, Charlie."

They exchanged stunned stares as the alarming realization of the seriousness of this warning sign sunk into their minds.

Braedon cleared his throat and coughed. "Let's get him home and bathe him."

"Yeah," Charity choked out, holding back her emotions. "Come on, Punkin, let's give you your last bath and brushing." The thought of doing something – anything at all for her childhood fur friend– was a comfort.

After Braedon untied a rope attached to the collar and crudely looped around the tree, he lifted the dog into his arms.

Charity placed a hand to the side of the canine's face, and in a strangled sob, she whispered, "I love you, baby."

They quietly trudged all the way to Charity's house. Once there, she removed the leather collar and ran warm water in the downstairs tub. Braedon lowered their beloved dog and began lovingly bathing him. They both dried him quickly with towels, and Charity ran the warm air from the hair dryer over the fur. Braedon held him on the back porch table for her to brush the dog's fur one last time. This act, too, comforted her. She and Braedon looked deeply into each other's eyes overtop of their old family friend, and he nodded before her arms surrounded the dog and gently hugged him to her chest one last time. They laid him down on the porch where he had liked to sleep so that Braedon could hurry to the shed for a wooden box that had once contained lamps when delivered and was still filled with bubble wrap. Charity brought out the blanket covering Punkin's breakfast-nook bed.

When Braedon had shoveled a space below the dog's favorite tree near the rock pond, they laid him to rest. Standing there in silence, once again, they clasped hands and squeezed. As they turned to walk to the porch, Braedon put a comforting arm around her shoulders. She clutched Punkin's collar to her heart.

"We have to report this to Bert, you know," he whispered.

She nodded as he fished his cell out of his back pocket.

When Officer Bertrand showed up with the young officer, he frowned at Braedon. "You mean to tell me you buried him already?" His voice had a hard edge to it. "Why, for cryin' out loud, didn't you call me as soon as you found him? I can't examine a dog and his surroundings after you've moved and buried him." He took his cap off to wipe his brow. "For Pete's sake, you even bathed him!" He yelled. Noticing the tears welling up in Charity's eyes and streaming down her cheeks, his tone softened. "All I'm sayin' is, I don't have anything to go on. I can't say he was hit by a stray bullet or deliberately shot. The chance of the last happening is a possibility. Especially since someone took an axe to our old boy not long ago." He put his cap back on his head. "Don't you see, Charity, even if I figured out who would do such a ghastly thing, I can't charge them with a crime." He leaned back on his heels, stretching his arms out at his side, and repeated, "I don't have anything to go on."

"I understand, Bert...Officer Bert. And I'm sorry. I just wanted to care for him and lay him to rest."

"We both did," Braedon confessed. "Calling the authorities didn't even occur to me until after we'd buried him. We didn't call anyone. Our girls don't know Punkin is gone yet, and they're going to be hurt to find out he's already buried without them being here."

Charity smiled through her tears. "I'd rather they remember Punkin the way he was when he was alive, anyway."

Lowering his arms to his sides, Officer Bertrand looked compassionately at both of these people he'd known as kids. He cleared his throat. "Well, I'll write up this report, too. But I won't trouble either of you anymore today." He turned to leave. "I'm really sorry this happened. Punkin was a good dog." He waved the younger officer to accompany him to the cruiser.

CHAPTER 15

As the days passed, Charity and Braedon concentrated on doing things with the girls, taking them to amusement parks, swimming pools, and sightseeing trips. Without saying a word about it, Charity began to think that maybe going back to the city was a good thing. Perhaps she needed to live elsewhere, to focus on her career... to escape the sorrow she had experienced in Country Lanes. She had had enough heartache for one lifetime. But each time she saw the yellow two-story house whenever they were driving back from one of their excursions with the girls, she remembered the love of her family and the companionship of friends, and her heart yearned for home.

On the last trip back home, almost as if picking up on Charity's quandary, Braedon suggested they call Florie and see if she would like the girls to spend another night and the next day with her while they explored the wine cellar.

"The wine cellar?" Charity asked. "You didn't want us to enter the wine cellar. Remember?" She turned her whole body toward him from the passenger seat. "You said it wasn't safe." She pointed an index finger at him. "Is this your way of enticing me to stay in this area longer, Bray?"

She could see in her peripheral vision that the girls had stopped their chattering and froze, wide-eyed.

Braedon cleared his throat. "N...Nooo..." He was obviously thinking up something. "The more I think about it, I'm certain we can at least enter the old stonework and at least see what kind of risks we would be taking. Aren't you just a little bit curious? I am, and I'd hate to do it alone after you're gone, knowing your interest."

"Now, Bray, you know I'm curious. We almost had a falling out because of my insatiable curiosity. Remember?"

"Yeah, unfortunately, I do remember."

At that, she felt ashamed. "I'm sorr-"

"Don't apologize again. It's over and done with, okay?"

Blushing, she turned back around in her seat. "You're right."

Despite her previous doldrums and the attempt to keep sorrow at bay by showing the girls a good time at the parks, by the next morning, Charity felt the stimulating pull of curiosity. No matter what web caught and suspended her spirit for agonizing moments at a time, she was always up for exploration, intrigue, and what she perceived as an adventure with a friend. In this case, she imagined heightened excitement if more than one friend joined their exploration. Having donned faded jeans and a worn sweatshirt, she had set out with Braedon and his opossum grin. Throwing her backpack on a stone slab near the pond, she put up a hand to stop Braedon from moving forward. "If you're still worried about our safety, why don't we call Cassie and Zak to join us?"

"But I packed everything, Charlie. Even a couple of lanterns. I'm armed with a pocket knife and everything."

"A pocket knife, eh? Well, if something falls on our head or a snake attacks, I suppose it might come in handy. But I think it would be nice to have a couple of other people to watch out for us or at least call for help if we need it."

Bray stopped in his tracks. "That might be the wisest thing, after all. They could camp out in front of the wine cellar in case we ran into trouble."

"Yeah," Charity's wheels were spinning again. "If we see it's safe enough in there and find anything interesting, they could come inside, too."

"Or we could take turns."

"Right. Or we could take turns."

They returned to the back porch to call Cassie's cell and hopefully have reason to wait for a while for friends to join them.

After what seemed like an interminably long period of time for Charity and Braedon, but was actually only twenty to thirty minutes, Cassie and Zak rounded the house to the back porch.

"Hey, girl, I'm glad you're dressed in ragged jeans and an old sweatshirt, too." Cassie blew her damp bangs away from her forehead. "You sure didn't give me time to change clothes," she declared pointedly.

Zak shook his head. "You really need to work on your scheduling skills, Charity Payne." He put his hands on the sides of the waistband of his grass-stained jeans and stood in a confrontational stance she knew was only a pose. "I was just about to change my mowing-grass clothes to go to Charleston." He tugged at his white t-shirt to demonstrate he'd been working so hard the material was sticking to his sweaty body.

"I'm sorry if I called at an inconvenient time, but-" She began apologizing until she noticed Zaks's wry grin. He wasn't buying her attempt at an earnest apology. "Oh, okay! I'm not sorry. I decided exploring the old wine cellar would be more fun with the two of you. So, at the last minute, I suggested to Bray that we call."

"Old wine cellar? On this property?" Zak's eyes scanned the meadow and the banks of the woods.

"Yes," Charity assured him. "It was covered up with so many vines and weeds we didn't recognize it for what it was at first. Bray and I ran across it when we were out hiking with Punkin." Her throat tightened as she said the dog's name, causing a strangled whisper.

Cassie put an arm around her shoulders. "I'm so sorry, Charlie. He was a wonderful dog and didn't deserve to go like that."

Zak exchanged knowing glances with Braedon. "We felt pretty bad when Braedon called and told us the news." He looked toward the base of the tree near the pond. "You laid him to rest by his favorite tree, didn't you, Charlie?"

She offered a nostalgic smile. "Yes, I figured he would like that familiar napping place." As Zak nodded and Cassie lowered her arm, Charity walked to the pond and picked her backpack up off the stone slab. "Okay, who's ready to explore an old wine cellar?"

She knew her friends caught on that she was changing the subject and attempting to shift the suddenly sad mood as much for their sakes as her own. In an effort of cooperation, they all exclaimed at once, "I am!"

By the time they reached the woods and followed the edge down to the creek, they were glad they wore hiking boots as they jumped and hopped flat rocks. Laughing at each other's clumsiness, they grabbed hands to scale the bank. They hiked through the woods in single file, their boots crunching and thudding through the dense, overhanging leaves and fallen twigs. Rabbits froze, stared, and then hopped quickly under brush, and squirrels scurried around and up into trees, peering down at these human invaders. When they finally reached their destination and stood in front of the old wine cellar, the amateur explorers surveyed its width and height, determining by the vine-covered openings that it actually had three arched stone entrances. In silent agreement, they pulled on work gloves and began to tug away dried vines as well as live clinging to some of the moss-covered stones. That task accomplished, they stood back in awe as Braeden snapped pictures.

"All right! We're ready to venture into this old ruin," he announced. "The middle entrance first since the original doors lie almost on the ground on the other openings, but someone must have reinforced that thick oak door in the center for some mysterious reason. It's going to take a lot of muscle to get it open after it's been shut for so long." He walked over and yanked the iron latch. "But, at least it's not padlocked." He turned toward them. "Are you guys as curious as I am?" He studied their faces. "Curious enough to band together to open this thing?"

"You got that right!" Zak exclaimed, nodding along with the women.

When the men forced back the latch, they all strained their muscles to work the thick door, managing – to their surprise – to open it farther than they expected.

"Okay, now." Braedon wiped the sweat off his brow with the back of a hand. "Charity and I will take my lantern inside first to get an idea of just how safe we think this cellar is. The lantern is charged up enough, so it should last for hours."

"I brought one, too, Bray," Charity informed him. "And it's also charged up in case we get trapped. See? You succeeded in putting the fear of adventure in me, after all!"

Zak rolled his eyes. "Well, it's about time *somebody* did, Charlie!" Spreading out two plastic mats, he motioned to Cassie, "Come on, Cas, let's sit down to *stand guard* while they get to go have fun."

"Fun, eh?" Charity raised her eyebrows and took an aggressive stance, hands on hips, and hovered over him as if challenging him face to face. "So you want to go first to make sure it's safe enough to explore? Huh?"

Zak glared at her. "I didn't say that. Don't get all snarky with me, Charity Payne. You asked me to come, and I dropped everything to please you, Ms. Snark!"

Charity's cheeks reddened. Uprighting herself, she felt the need to apologize to this good friend for her unwarranted confrontation. "I'm sorry, Zak. You don't deserve my short-tempered reaction. We're not kids anymore." She realized she had automatically slipped back in time when they had sniped verbally at each other. "You did drop everything you'd planned, and I wouldn't have blamed you if you hadn't come at such short notice. I appreciate you and Cas, both, for giving up your own plans for mine."

A soft squeeze on her upper arm from Braedon's hand quieted her for a moment. Shame for her angry outburst forced heat to spread from her neck into her face. She shook her head. "I really am sorry, Zak. I don't know why I'm reverting to the behavior of a spoiled brat."

"Not a spoiled brat, Charlie. Just a bull-headed brat," Zak responded before Cassie ran her hand down the middle of his back in an attempt to calm him. He glanced back at his sister. "I should say headstrong." Turning toward Charity, he added, "And that is a good trait to have in some cases...I think." When Cassie scooted closer beside him, nudged his side with an elbow, and bit her lower lip, his face reddened. "I'm sorry, too, Charlie. You would think I'd matured more through the years than to spout off petty comments. The truth is I thought that Braedon and I should investigate the conditions inside the old cellar before you women entered. That's all. But, instead of explaining that to you, I came off sounding petty and resentful."

Charity bent down to place a hand on his shoulder. "I didn't stop to wonder how you felt, Zak. I jumped into that old sparring mode with both verbal fists flying. It was crazy." She stood up, facing the middle entrance of the old ruin. "But I still want to explore the cellar with Braedon. We need a couple of people out here in case something should collapse."

Looking up at her, Zak nodded. "I understand. And we'll be here for you, Charlie."

Charity leaned down again for a hug. "Thank you," she whispered.

Zak and Cassie looked at her sympathetically before both grasped her hands as in their youthful past after a fuss, and all three stated emphatically, "Friends."

Braedon and Charity checked their water supply, each enjoying a swig before slowly advancing toward the cave cellar's middle entrance. Leaving the other lantern behind, Braedon held the light up high in front of them as they stopped just inside the opening. They gave their eyes time to adjust to the darkness and the spread of the hand-held illumination. Charity thought it a good thing they had when her vision focused on large barrels practically in front of her. The huge containers were dirty and jutted out on either side, leaving only a narrow path between them. However had the workers managed to install them so close together? Touching the first one and attempting to shake it with both hands, she guessed they were empty. Moving forward in the dark, they surveyed the stone ceiling and felt a slight chill. Inching along and distracted by their own shadows hovering with every step, Braedon swung the lantern even higher with one hand while he pointed to another arched doorway at the end of the passageway. It occurred to Charity that they were refraining from speaking aloud as if the ghosts of the past would hear them intruding into their now private cellar. But instead of an exit against the mountain, they encountered a second room ahead of them. Stone slabs supporting oak shelves lined the walls on both sides. Under each slab, a cabinet protruded. Toward the end of the room, floor to ceiling, a full-size cabinet similar to a wardrobe stirred their restrained curiosity. A long oak table, bare except for inches of grime and dust, set in the middle of the room. They separated to slide by the table, seeing the third doorway. A makeshift door built of thinner wood and cut to fit the arched opening held a latch and lock. Since the wood was old and the lock rusted, Braedon was able to break off the latch itself. Charity, feeling a rush of heightened curiosity and confidence at this point, impulsively hurried past Braedon into the next room and ran smack into something cold hanging from the ceiling. She let out a scream capable of creating a cave-in, backing into her confused companion as the lantern lit up a dark lifeless snake.

"Whoa, whoa, Charlie!" He caught her arm. "Take it easy, girl. It's okay. It's dead." He let go of her and reached out his hand to pat it. "See?"

"It scared me when it hit me in the face!"

"It didn't hit you, Charlie. You ran past me into the dark, head first, and hit it."

"Well, whatever. It frightened me!"

He looked down into her face in wonder. "That's the first time I ever heard you admit to fright."

"Oh, come on!" She crept close to his side, "Let's just take care it doesn't happen again."

She could sense his grin all the way through to her bones, but ignored it.

Stone slabs and oak shelves stuck out from the walls, but these weren't empty. It suddenly dawned upon both of them that they held ancient artifacts. There they sat as if wary of discovery. Effigy pipes – bears, birds, small animals, frogs, turtles, as well as a few tubular stone pipes. Human effigies stared at the interlopers. Beaded and shell necklaces lay stretched out. Copper bracelets and full-face masks glowed in the artificial light: stone axes, spears, stones shaped for grinding, and arrowheads of different sizes. Three shelves displayed pottery – some chipped or cracked, some whole, some plain, and others with checkered-like marks. The couple gaped at an amazing variety of small engraved stone tablets. The marks on several of these looked like chicken scratchings, but other tablets drew attention by their deeply penetrated marks, appearing to have order.

Charity squeezed Braedon's arm. "These couldn't have come from the same burial mound, Bray. Look at that copper helmet with attached ear pieces."

"I know, Char. There's everything here from green slag slate, copper, and iron. Do you realize what this means?"

As they once again inched forward, she whispered. "I don't even know what every item is or what it was used for."

Shining the light toward the end of the room, they gasped in shock. On a big table lay a huge breastplate and the largest and heaviest stone ax they had ever seen.

"What in the world...." Charity uttered.

Braedon couldn't say anything for a moment, and then, he croaked a quote, "And there were giants in the earth in those days...."

Charity stared in awe and nodded. "Genesis 6:4."

Creeping footsteps sounded somewhere behind them, but as they turned in surprise, the light revealed nothing. Both straining to see beyond the edge of darkness, they spotted an eerie light approaching from the second room. A loud feminine whisper echoed, "Charity?"

A gruffer voice called, "Braedon? Where are you, Buddy?"

"I'm here!" Braedon called back.

Zak's body, magnified by the light, and looming shadows filled the doorway.

"Hey, move it, Zak! It's getting too dark in here!" Cassie gently pushed her brother out of the way. As her brother ducked around the hanging snake, she scolded them. "We got worried about you two when you didn't show up to tell us it was safe in here."

Braedon bit his lower lip in a grimace and hung his head.

Charity piped up, " Ohhh... sorry, Cas. We got carried away the further we explored."

"Well, at least you're okay and still standing." With both lanterns lighting the area, she noticed the artifacts. "Hey, what's all this?"

Zak drew near the shelves, fingering a few of the relics, and whistled. "Motherload!" He and Cassie let their eyes roam over the room. "Are these things out of a mound?"

Charity lowered her voice, "I strongly suspect more than one mound. And you're *not* to tell anyone until we decide what to do. Understand?"

"My lips are sealed," her best friend promised.

"And you, Zak?" Braedon's tone demanded an answer.

"Me, too. The epitome of discretion," Zak stated.

It was when Charity and Braedon stepped aside that the siblings caught sight of the breastplate. They stopped talking and ran their hands down the front of it in amazement.

Braedon coughed, and motioned for them all to turn around and backtrack to the entrance.

Having exited, they stood, each in awe at what was hidden inside that above-ground stone cellar. "I know someone who can help us decide what to do with this find." Charity kept her voice level though excitement bubbled up. "Professor Norton."

Giving that some thought, they all nodded their heads.

"Uh oh," Cassie uttered. "What time is it, Zak?"

Zak glanced at his watch. "Going on three."

"Oh no! We'll be late for Mother's birthday dinner if we don't hurry to the house and get cleaned up." Looking through the woods, she added, "I'm so sorry, Charlie. I completely forgot about Mother's birthday, and with Dad gone...."

"Don't worry about it, Cas. I understand. Thank you for coming! Now scoot!"

The siblings waved bye to them as they headed out of the woods.

"Well, that leaves just you and me, kid." Braedon switched off the lanterns. "Let's grab a late lunch in your breakfast nook."

Charity held up an index finger. "And then, we'll go see the History professor."

He winked at her. "Gotcha!"

Neither seemed to notice their environment as they walked trance-like, lost-in-thought and mental images, out of the woods, across the creek, through a field until they reached the house. As they munched on cold baloney sandwiches and chips followed by sips of iced tea, they talked about certain ancient pieces of interest.

The afternoon sun pelted them with heat as they approached Florie's garage apartment. They stopped for only a few moments to check on the girls and see if the professor was there. In confidence, they told Charity's aunt what they had found and why they needed her friend.

The couple strode with purpose up the paved walk to the steps of the old mansion rising majestically with its round tower. It didn't take too long for Julia Norton to come to the door dressed in a long tunic splashed with swirls of bright colors and distressed jeans. She greeted them with one of her beautiful, toothy smiles.

"Hello there! I think you two are the second visitors to come to my new abode!" Her smile faded just as quickly. "I hope nothing's wrong with Florie."

"No, no," Charity quickly assured her. "She seems much improved. No, we came to share a discovery that might interest you... if you don't mind."

" A discovery?" Merely the word itself had this intelligent woman intrigued. "Don't mind?! I'm delighted you thought of me! Come inside for a breath of AC, and let's talk discovery!"

Sitting on the thickly stuffed couch layered with colorful throws, they told her of uncovering the wine cellar and of their stupendous find while exploring the stone structure.

"And that is why we thought you would like to see these artifacts for yourself," Braedon ventured.

Charity placed a hand on his arm. "Actually, since you've studied and taught history and participated in digs, you may be able to tell us something about the artifacts and help us decide what to do about them."

Julia's brown eyes had widened throughout the account of their discovery. It was obvious she was practically drooling over the prospect of this find, but was maintaining her professional composure. After all, they weren't here on a social call, but requesting her aid and knowledge as a professor and archaeological digger. Her excitement betrayed her as she exclaimed, "Well, what are we waiting for? Let me go up to the tower and get my brother and pull on my boots, and we're outta here!"

The couple looked around at their surroundings, taking in the dark woodwork and staircase. Admiring the antique tables, they noticed a postcard lying on one of the end tables. It looked very familiar with its cut-out letters. Charity picked it up and read aloud in a low voice meant only for Braedon's ears. "I know why you're here. Go back where you came from." They stared at each other in dismay.

Julia came running down the stairs and swung open the coat closet to grab her boots, but stopped when she saw Charity's stunned expression as she stood holding the postcard. "Sorry you had to see that. I should've put it in a drawer or the trash." She shook her head. "Somebody doesn't want us here, and made it clear."

"Where did you get this?" Braedon questioned.

"Somebody slipped it between my front door and the frame while I was at Florie's house. My brother must have been napping or taking a shower. He said he didn't see anyone."

Charity and Braedon nodded, but were quiet as Julia sat down in an overstuffed chair and pulled on her leather boots. Their eyelids lowered as they peeked at one another.

Boots stomping on the steps caused them all to look toward the stairs as a khaki-clad man with dark skin and grizzled white hair and beard descended. His brows frowned at Charity, who still held the postcard.

"Jessey, this is the young woman I told you about, Florie's niece, Charity. Charity, my brother Jessey, the anthropologist."

A big toothy smile, much like his sister's, stretched her brother's handsome face, accentuating his chocolate brown eyes. "Former anthropologist. Pleased to meet you, Charity." He took the postcard from her with one hand while shaking her hand with the other.

"Glad to meet you, too, Dr. Norton."

"Jessey, please."

"Okay. Jessey." She managed a smile.

In spite of unasked questions, the four hurried in anticipation as they left the house. A movement caught Charity's attention, and out of the corner of her eye, she spotted Roy viewing the birds through binoculars from his Victorian's back steps on a distant hill. Aunt Florie and the girls waved from her porch as they all passed in high spirits of adventure.

Charity and Braedon grabbed their backpacks, lanterns, and bottles of water at the house before the four of them headed across the creek.

Julia's dark eyes gleamed as she stood in front of the wine cellar. And her cheekbones glistened as she flattened a hand on the wide and weathered stones. "This is one of those wine cellars in operation only about three years before the civil war broke out. Swiveling on her heels, she gazed over the wooded expanse behind her. "Do you see those terraced sections running the length of the property below us? They have the dried up remains of cultivated grape vines, intermingled with weeds, wild bushes, and flowers – now worthless, but probably very productive back then." They squinted, trying to perceive what she was able to envision. "There is even more history to these cave cellars in this area during the civil war."

Since the couple looked at her quizzically and attentively, she continued as she pointed to the aged structure. "They were often used as an underground railroad."

"Railroad?" Charity asked.

"Freedom," Jessey stated as Julia nodded.

Understanding, Charity looked at the wine cellar with even more respect. "Well, this one found another use *after* the Civil War. Come inside and see for yourself, if you don't mind cobwebs. But watch out for barrels sticking out and a certain dead snake still hanging from the roof."

Julia and her brother exchanged amused glances.

They all crept carefully through the dark, cool rooms, lighting their steps with the sway of lantern light and looming shadows. This time, Charity remembered to dodge the flattened snake hanging in the front of the third room. Jessey, however, simply tugged, adjusted his grip, and pulled the snake down. Charity looked back at the cellar floor, half expecting the snake to come to life and attack in revenge or slither away in appreciation for his rescue. Of course, none of that happened. It lay lifeless as ever and harmless.

The ancient artifacts set undisturbed, waiting and calling to them to ponder their mysteries.

Julia didn't utter a word as she slowly inched along the tables, her brother close to her heels, sometimes lifting pottery bowls and, sometimes, fingering beautiful crystal beads, carved necklaces, or copper bracelets. However, she came to a dead stop in front of the breastplate. She and her brother exchanged amazed looks.

"Do you see this, Julia?!" Jessey exclaimed. "A large copper head plate and ear attachments! The one who wore this armor was pretty sizable, wouldn't you say?"

"What *is* your professional opinion, Professor Norton?" Charity was obviously anxious for her to say something or at least react.

Julia licked her lips, gone dry from viewing such a large and varied collection. "One thing I can say without sitting down and studying each piece, is that these artifacts were collected from various sources. She pointed to a bowl with criss-cross markings. "This, for instance, probably was uncovered at a Kentucky site. I'm seeing some that I think were taken from Ohio mounds. And-"

"*And* they're all mine!" A gruff voice bellowed.

CHAPTER 16

All four swung around in shock. Roy took a defensive stance a couple of yards away, his binoculars dangling from the strap around his neck and a rifle trained on them.

When Braedon growled, "Now see here, Roy," Charity placed a warning hand on his arm.

"What are you doing, Roy?" She deliberately kept her composure and a steady voice, hoping to defuse the situation.

"Claimin' what's mine! That's what!" He glared at her. "And no-body's gonna stop me! You hear?! My great-grandfather owned this land and put these things in here himself. Nobody is gonna take away my inheritance!"

"So now you want to pull a gun on us, your friends? Instead of examining what is actually here?"

Roy's eyes darted around the room. "You knew they were on this land the whole time. Didn't you, Charity, girl? That's why you bought the shovel and rake and...and...visited the museum. To see what you'd be lookin' for. You don't fool me one bit!"

"No, I didn't know, Roy. I honestly didn't know."

Roy sneered. "Yeah, right. Jus' plain ol' coincidence. Right."

She sent up a silent prayer to keep her voice from trembling as she tried to explain. "No. We're working on an article about the mounds for a magazine. And we just discovered the wine cellar a few days ago." A perplexed expression crossed his face. She discerned that he was attempting to assimilate this information. She paused, letting the words sink into his confused mind. She mentally sent up another prayer for God to deliver them from this dangerous threat. "I don't plan to keep any of these items."

He shot her a dubious look. With the gun shaking, he let his eyes scan the collection. "Where's the gold? And the jewels? The gems? What did you do with that stuff?"

"Gold?"

"Yeah, where'd you hide the gold things and the gems?"

"We haven't run across anything made from gold. And the only stones we've seen so far are small tablets with etchings."

"Come on. The parchment says, *treasure*. Where's the treasure?"

Charity confused him further, when putting the puzzle pieces together, she couldn't resist a smile. "Roy, to a professional archaeologist and amateur archaeologist or merely a collector with a great appreciation for relics of ancient civilizations, uncovered artifacts *are* a treasure."

Roy's shoulders drooped, and his hands lowered the gun a few inches, but he quickly raised it again. "This is all your fault, Charity. I tried everything to get you to leave."

"Including taking the water pipes apart?"

"Nah, my nephew did that. But it was my idea. I thought you would leave the house."

"Did he lock Punkin in the old shed?"

"Nope, I did that, myself."

Charity maintained her calm demeanor. "You sneaked the post-cards under the door."

"Again, my nephew. But I put them together." A smug sneer crossed his face.

"Why Julia and her brother?"

"Hmm, a mystery, ain't it? Are you naïve or somethin', Charity, or are you jus' a good actress?" Roy raised his eyebrows, staring at her pointedly. "A History professor and an anthropologist? Both spent summers on digs? Quite a coincidence, they'd move into our little community, not too far away from my land. Maybe...just maybe...I put two and two together and came up with four." He smirked.

Charity stalled for time. "Think about it, Roy. A History professor who has taught in our region for years and developed friendships. She simply settled into a house of historical value when she retired. It just happened to be in our area."

"Yeah...uh huh... tell me another one. That one doesn't hold wa-ter."

"Put that darn gun down, Roy," Another deep male voice de-manded. Lowering the rifle to the ground, Roy jerked around to face Carter Grant, who aimed a twenty-two at his face. "You jus' leave these good-hearted people alone and go home before you get into boilin' hot water." When Roy didn't move, Carter asked a pointed question. "What were you gonna do, Roy? Shoot'em all?"

The man's eyes rounded as he gave the question some thought. "Nah...to tell you the truth, I hadn't got that far yet in my plans. Everything happened so fast. I knew somethin' was up when Charity and Braedon were rushin' to Julia's house...the very people who want-ed to run off with my great-grandfather's stuff. I figured it out, then. They were all in it together. I guess I wanted to scare them real bad."

Carter's face hardened. "Any action you might take would be a crime, Roy."

"Carter," Roy stated, dropping the gun. "You're jus' hangin' on to that crush you had on Alice all these years."

"By golly, I promised to take care of her property. And, mister, I'm lookin' out for her daughter, too." He picked up the gun, lowering his own. Shoving his face close to Roy's, meeting him eye to eye, he snarled, " And I don't turn my back on old friends for a few extra bucks."

Something snapped in Roy Galligher. Tears spilled out of his eyes as if scales had popped off, releasing an overflow. He fell to his knees as Carter stepped back. "My, Lord, what's come over me?! Please forgive me, God!"

Braedon couldn't hold back his anger any longer. "It's called greed, Galligher. The spirit of greed."

Charity eased next to the broken man and knelt. "Hey, Roy, of course God forgives you. We're all susceptible to the temptation of greed and other sins the demons dangle in front of our human faces. It's a spiritual battle we don't always win right away. That's why the Shepherd uses the crook on his staff to pull His own sheep out of the pit or from the cliff's edge. Other times, his staff prods us in the right direction whether we heed His guidance or not. But He is always aware of the deceiving spirits and ready to forgive when we confess and turn back to Him." She patted his back. "You haven't hurt anyone, Roy."

He raised his head, pain in his eyes. "Yes, I have. I've hurt you." An anguished sob tore through his words. "And I've hurt Punkin."

Charity swallowed a hard lump in her throat. Her voice came out weak and strangled. "Punkin? *You?*" Her eyes darted around the cellar in shock. Trying to control her racing heart and focus on his face, she whispered, "You've known and loved Punkin almost as long, and as much as I have, Roy."

His eyes met hers. "Yep, I loved him, Charity. He was a good dog. I had to stop and wipe my eyes when it came time to put him down." Roy held out his hands. "He stood and looked affectionate the way he always did. You know? He wagged his tail and sat down on his haunches like he was posin' for the kill."

Charity's heart beat faster before it plopped and twisted into her stomach. "He thought you were taking a picture of him." Through a blur of unshed tears, she saw Braedon shaking his head as his chest heaved and one of his hands balled into a fist. Carter swiped the deeply rutted creases on his face. Her voice took on a pleading tone as if the unbelievable hadn't happened yet. "Why did you shoot him, Roy? He didn't have many more years to spend with me."

Sorrow pooled Roy's eyes. "I know, sweetheart. I'm sorry. He gave chase every time my nephew snuck around to try to break into the house to find the certificate of sale of the land. At first, I tried to find it after the funeral when everybody was gone, but wasn't doin' that good. So I got my nephew to agree to search for it." Attempting to justify his actions, Roy continued in vain, "The courthouse had burned, but the way your mother acted, I figured a copy existed somewhere in the house. I reasoned I could destroy it, and no one could prove a sale even took place." Perspiration broke out on his forehead at the admission. "I didn't want to, Charity. I swear to you. But he said he would quit and go home if I didn't get rid of that dog. I even put him in that old shed at the end of my property and fed him when I wrestled with the problem." He grasped her hands. "I'm so sorry, Charity. Please forgive me. I don't blame you if you can't. Jus' know I'm truly grieved over this thing. If it's any comfort to ya, Punkin laid his head over on the tree and looked like he'd just gone to sleep."

Picturing the sad scene, she swallowed but managed to squeeze his hands. "I'll get through this, Roy... somehow...and you will, too."

It was clear by his red face and steely eyes that it would take Braedon a longer period of time to work out his anger. "Did you hit him in the head with an ax, Roy?" He looked like he wanted to tear off the man's head.

"No! Of course not!" Roy bellowed. "My nephew was supposed to jus' scare Charity. He went too far. I bawled him out good when I found out what he'd done." Meeting Braedon's belligerent stare, he stated, "I would never have hurt that dog like that."

"You *killed* that dog, Roy!" Braedon spat out.

"It was a clean, quick shot!" Roy declared. Lowering his head, he muttered, as an afterthought to his justification, "Once I brought myself to do it, that is. I tell you, he went peacefully."

Julia and her brother had stood tensely silent in the back all this time. She pulled her phone out of her jacket pocket. "The police are on the way."

Charity looked at Roy's tear-stained face and quivering lips, seeing only her parents' old friend. With tears welling up in her eyes again as she thought of what he had done, she managed to breathe a whisper. "The police?"

"Yes. My long nimble digger fingers texted a message to our friend Officer Bertrand. The department tried to call, but I'd silenced my phone. In all the commotion, it vibrated, but I didn't answer."

When the police finally showed up, the day was waning, and they were all outside the wine cellar. Responding to a warning glare from Charity, Braedon, Carter and the other two kept tight-lipped and quiet. Charity gave Roy a stern opportunity to surrender himself.

Roy hung his head until he blurted, "I held a rifle on these people." He waved his arms and hands toward those standing behind him.

Officer Bertrand raised his eyebrows in disbelief. "Roy?"

"Yeah, I did, Bert. All for the artifacts hoarded by my great-grand-father on land I considered still belonged to my family." He hung his head again. "It doesn't. It legally belongs to Charity here. But my mind couldn't or wouldn't accept that fact." Roy rubbed his forehead. "I believed I was entitled to the artifacts my ancestor had gathered. My stupid greed wanted anything gold or inlaid with jewels."

Officer Bert had known all these individuals for years, except the Nortons, but he had even befriended them when he had paid a visit to welcome Julia and her brother to Country Lanes. "You know it's my duty to take you in, Roy, and get your full statement."

Roy raised his head in determination. "Well, speakin' of full, that's not all."

Bert's bushy, gray eyebrows raised over his Irish blue eyes.

"You can add dog killin' to the charges."

"Dog killin'?"

"Yeah, I shot the best dog in the world," Roy choked out. "I shot and killed Charity's dog."

"Old Punkin? You actually shot Punkin? Why on earth wou-"

"It's a long story. A long, stupid story."

Officer Bert thumped him on the back. "Sorry, Buddy, but I do have to take you in, and you'll have plenty of time to tell me that long story." He handcuffed Roy, but didn't lead him by the arm. He knew his long-time friend would follow.

"Well, take me, too, Bert," Carter piped up.

"You? You in on this, Carter?"

"Nope. But I held my .22 on Roy."

"This is getting stranger and stranger. Crazy!" The officer was writing on a pad as fast as he could. "Come on, then. Gotta hear this whole story. I figure your act was in defense, so you'll just have to come with me."

Startled, Roy's swollen, bloodshot eyes narrowed, and his bottom lip overlapped his upper one. He sent a distrustful glance Carter's way.

The older man, still carrying both guns, lowered his eyes to the ground when he passed the weapons to another officer. He kicked at a rock with the toe of his scuffed-up boot. "Come on, Roy. Let's go down together. Jus' two ol' friends walkin' and talkin' like we used to. Right, Roy?"

Understanding passed between the two men, and Roy nodded.

They all walked through the woods, following the officers up a different and longer path than they had taken in the search for the wine cellar. They moved in the solemnity usually reserved for a funeral procession. While everyone else headed for the back porch or the cruiser in the driveway, Charity stopped by the tree near the rock pond.

Roy fell behind, easing beside her. "Is this where you laid Punkin to rest?"

She only nodded.

A huge sigh escaped him before he could control it. "It was always a favorite spot for him."

Her gaze cleared and focused on his face. "I'll be honest with you, Roy. It hurts to know how he passed away...by the hand of someone he and I both trusted. I want you to know the hurt cuts deep." Tears ran down her cheeks. "I wasn't with him. I didn't get to say goodbye."

"I know." His own eyes glazed with tears. "I can't tell you enough how sorry I am, sweetheart. I don't know what got into me." He couldn't wipe the tears that streamed because his hands were cuffed. "If I could go back...if I could turn back time, please, believe me, I would."

She raised a hand and patted his shoulder. "I believe you, Roy. I think you really would."

As the cruiser backed up and pulled away with the two forlorn men in the back seat, the remaining friends walked to the front of the house and stood, watching it disappear down the road.

Braedon gulped the fresh air. "Let's take a slow, deep breath and let the tension go, okay?"

Julia held a thumb under her chin and the index finger above her upper lip in thought. "I can call my contacts, the right people with expertise, Charity, to take charge of the collection. They'll do the inventory and assess these artifacts if that is all right with you."

"I would appreciate it, Julia. Thank you."

"I'm going to take Julia and her brother home and pick up the girls at Florie's. Is there anything I can get you, Charity?" Braedon offered.

"No, not really. I just need a little time alone."

"I tell you what, folks," Braedon smiled knowingly. "I'll take the girls home with me tonight, but let's all get together tomorrow evening around the fire pit. I'll even grill some steaks to celebrate our great discovery. What do you say?"

Charity had to forgive his attempt to change the somber atmosphere. "I'll invite Cassie and Zak," Charity offered, trying to lift herself out of the murky hole that wanted to sink her heart.

"How 'bout I bring my sis, Livie?" Braedon suggested. "She would enjoy another campfire with company."

"And I'll bring your Aunt Florie!" Julia suggested. "It'll do her good to get out of the house after staying home all this time."

"Thank you, Julia. I'll make side dishes to go with the steaks."

"And I'll make desserts."

When everyone was gone, and Charity sat on the back porch, sipping her favorite raspberry-flavored coffee from a mug, she remembered how Braedon had whispered in her ear, reminding her that he was taking the girls home with him to give her time to unwind. *He knows me so well.* The girls would want to invite Nick to this cookout, and this, too, would be fine with her. Meanwhile, she would sit here watching the sunset's yellow-orange spread through the sky and transcend into twilight's rosy glow.

Just you and me, Punkin.

CHAPTER 17

Toward morning Charity heard rain pelting the windows and wondered if they would be able to have the cookout after all. If not, they would prepare food in the house, but she thought it was much more fun and relaxing to sit around the fire pit and have the men take turns at the grill. Listening to the patter of raindrops on the roof, she fell back off to sleep.

A beautiful afternoon awaited them as Braedon and the girls pulled up early in preparation for the cookout. It wasn't long until the girls, dressed in colorful hoodies and capris, were begging to go after their friend Nick. Adrianna and Willow skipped off down the road as Olivia made a beeline for one of the rockers, her earbuds attached to her phone. Braedon encouraged Charity to take a walk with him as they stood at the end of the driveway watching the girls run out of sight.

"I'm not dressed for a walk, Bray. I'm wearing a dress and sandals. I have only a shawl ready to cover my shoulders if the temp drops. You're the one wearing jeans, a t-shirt, and boots!"

"We're not going hiking, Charlie. Just a nice stroll together. The tiny flowers on your pretty dress will fit in just fine, I promise you." Tilting his head lower, letting a lock of hair fall onto his forehead, he peeked at her through his lashes, his face reddening. "Besides, it's our only chance to be alone before everyone shows up."

"You want to be alone with me?" she teased, moving close to him.

He grinned. "I confess. I do." With one arm swinging around her waist, he cupped her chin with his other hand and gently brushed her lips with his. What was meant as a brief act of affection melted upon contact into a deeper kiss full of pent-up emotion between them.

Catching her breath, Charity stepped away from the circle of his arms. A wisp of movement near the incline toward the woods distracted her from further conversation. She barely felt Braedon's touch on her arm as he followed her line of vision and also detected motion in that direction. The summer breeze ruffled the fur of a dog sitting at a distance, staring down at the couple. A white streak from the top of the brown fur on his head to his black nose sparkled in the spotlight of sunshine. He stood up, pawing the ground with his white paws as if in anticipation.

"Punkin?" Charity whispered. Before Braedon could stop her, she practically glided across the yard and uphill, her blond hair swaying in the breeze. The creature leaped in excitement and pranced to meet her. As he flew into her outstretched arms, she had a bitter-sweet realization that he wasn't her beloved Punkin, but a younger version.

Nick, fully dressed in jeans and a red sweatshirt for the cookout, loped up to both of them. "Sorry, Ms. Payne. I thought he'd follow me, not run ahead into you first."

Still hugging the dog, she laughed in joy. "Is this your dog, Nick?"

"Yes and no. He's one of the pups born to our family's dog Macie."

"He looks so much like Punkin!"

"That's because Punkin was the daddy."

Charity squatted, looking deeply into the dog's eyes. The canine responded by licking her cheek.

"What's his name?"

"He doesn't have one yet. Mom says if I don't find a home for him, he goes to the no-kill shelter and givin' him a name wouldn't be fair to him." The boy's cheeks colored as Charity rose to her feet. "I was hopin'...well, I hoped..."

"You hoped what, Nick?"

"I was hopin' you'd take him, seein' how he looks so much like Punkin and all, and I'd get to see him from time to time...and-" The boy stopped as something suddenly occurred to him. "Uh...that is... if you and Adrianna plan to stay in Country Lanes."

Braedon moved beside Charity and grasped her hand. They searched each other's eyes.

The girls rushed up. "We're not going anywhere, are we, Mom?" Adrianna asked anxiously.

"Oh, please, say you'll stay, Charity! *Please!*" Willow pleaded. "Adrianna is my best friend, and I'm not going anywhere!" Braedon's daughter inhaled a fresh breath of air. "Are we, Daddy?"

He studied these anxious faces before turning to Charity. "Hmm, it all depends. What are you going to do, Charity?"

She, too, studied the eager faces that waited in suspense for her answer. Gazing into Braedon's questioning eyes, she whispered. "Staying."

Braedon exhaled the breath he held. "Well, it's settled. We're staying, too."

The kids started jumping, yelling at full lung capacity, and hugging each other. Punkin Junior, yet to have an official name of his own, barked into the boisterous laughter.

"Okay!" Braedon hooted. "Now, we have something to really celebrate! Let's get this cookout set up before company comes!"

"Do you think the grass will be dry enough by then, Bray?" Charity asked.

"The way the sun is already beating down on us, I'd say it won't take long," he assured her.

Arm in arm, Braedon and Charity followed the happy youngsters down the slope toward the back of the house. Eliciting chuckles, the dog squeezed his way between the couple, and then trotted contentedly in front of them. Suddenly, something caught Braedon's attention out of the corner of his eye. As he half-turned, he squinted into the sun toward the top of the bank to see what looked like a dog: ears perked up, brown fur ruffled by the breeze. Braedon rubbed his eyes with the back of a hand and squinted again at the creature. White streaked from the canine's intensely focused brown eyes to the edge of his black nose. The dog sat down, the fur on his white chest puffing out majestically, and raised a white paw.

"What is it, Bray?" Charity stopped and tried to follow his gaze.

His head swiveled in her direction. "Do you see that?" His low voice held a note of awe.

"Do I see what?"

Turning back, he whispered, "Do you see that..." There was nothing there. Just brush, tall grass, and wildflowers waving in the wind.

Her eyes searched the bank and the edge of the woods. "Do I see what?"

Looking disappointed, he shook his head. "Nothing. I guess it was an optical illusion."

They slowly trailed the kids to the back of the house, Braedon still lost in thought.

"Hey, look, ya'll!" Willow exclaimed, pointing to the sky.

A rainbow spread its colorful arch across the heavens.

Braedon nodded and uttered, "Goodbye, Punkin, boy."

Charity sent Braedon a knowing smile. "Goodbye, baby," she whispered.

Shaking himself out of his preoccupation, Braedon yelled. "You know what, kids?!" He had their full attention. "I think this is a good time to read about Noah and the flood!"

He extended his hand upward. "And how God put a rainbow in the sky as a reminder of a promise to man."

They all stood gazing at the beautiful rainbow, mindful of its significance.

Charity slipped her hand into the warmth of Braedon's strong hand. The look she gave him was one of pent-up love. His eyes answered with a spark of hope.

ABOUT AUTHOR

A Poet and Storyteller, Shirley Hedrick Williams was born in Charleston, West Virginia; and spent her childhood in the Charleston area. She began writing short stories at the age of 11. Shirley has published poems in Journals across America through the years and received the title of A West Virginia Ambassador of Poetry for All Peoples as a Member of the West Virginia Poetry Society from the Secretary of State, A. James Manchin in April 1984.

Having worked in a library for 12 years, she knows what readers enjoy from a good story. Recently, she has moved her focus to writing Christian Romantic Suspense novels that take place in West Virginia or the Carolinas.

Shirley is married and the mother of two grown children – a daughter and a son – both writers. She enjoys trips to scenic mountains, woodlands, and rivers with her family, but her heart will always lie in the hills of West Virginia.

Connect with her at ShirleyHedrickWilliams @ fireandgracepubl ishing.com

OTHER BOOKS FROM SHIRLEY HEDRICK WILLIAMS

Don't forget to check out other books from Shirley Hedrick Williams and FIRE and GRACE Publishing, LLC

Releasing Shadows (A Christian Inspirational Romance)

Awakening Crow Moon: and Other Poems and Short Stories